2 -

Copyright ©2019 C.G. Oster
All rights reserved.

This is a work of fiction. Names, characters, places, and incidents are the work of the author's imagination, or are used fictitiously, and any resemblance to actual persons, living or dead, business establishments, locales, or events is entirely coincidental.

Mischief

In

St. Tropez

Dory Spark Mysteries Book 2

By Camille Oster

Mischief in St. Tropez

Chapter 1

Covering her eyes with her hand, Dory stared out at the bright, glittering Mediterranean sea. The blue water married with the sky in the distance and a warm sea breeze rustled her skirt. She sighed and turned around to walk back up the vast garden covering the rough terrain at the edge of Lady Pettifer's property.

They had nothing planned for the day, which were Dory's favorite kind of days. Livinia, Lady Pettifer's niece, was at home too, but would most likely dash off to Cannes by the afternoon to seek the company of her friends. Who wanted to be in sleepy, old St. Tropez when the soirees never stopped an hour's drive away?

After initial misgivings, Livinia had grown to love it here on the coast. Granted, she would prefer being closer to the lively towns of Cannes or Nice, but she'd found her set, and they were a wild and varied bunch. Dory liked it here too, although she preferred the more sedate lifestyle of this small fishing village.

Over the last year and a half, her French was perfected and she knew the butcher, the baker and the candlestick maker. In fact, she knew everyone in the village. They weren't, by far, the only Brits here, but it was a certain set that lived out in these smaller villages, and they weren't Livinia's set.

In saying that, the coast in general was now more replete than it had been when Dory had first arrived. The Americans had mostly left, leaving only the more hardy

Brits, returning the Cote de Azur to how it used to be in the twenties—exactly how Lady Pettifer loved it. There had always been the British Colony here, but the young, bright and rich Americans had come and ever so gently pushed them out.

That withstanding, it was hard to even recognize that they were officially at war. There had been widespread panic, when in the autumn, both England and France had declared war on Germany. Since then, nothing had happened and life had effectively returned to normal. Even the Duke and Duchess of Windsor were still staying here on the coast. It was the war that never happened.

Obviously, things were more complicated than that, but not here in the endless spring sunshine. People got on with their business and the parties were thrown like they always had been.

Reaching the top of the stairs, Dory put her hat on before crossing the expanse of lawn around Lady Pettifer's villa. She didn't have skin that took the sun well—she burned to a crisp if she wasn't careful. It was a hard lesson she'd learnt to her own misery in her first few weeks here.

Looking comfortable, Lady Pettifer sat in the seating area under a vine leaf covered pergola, a tea service steaming in front of her.

"There you are, dear," Lady Pettifer said. "Any dolphins today?"

"I didn't see any," Dory said as she sat down. She could use a cup. Music started playing upstairs in the house, leeching out of open windows as the breeze shifted. They both looked up at the open window above them. "Livinia is still here, I see."

"I understand Richard is picking her up in an hour." Richard Dormstry was one of Livinia's friends, who essentially did whatever she wished. He drove an hour to pick her up, then an hour back. Everyone saw that Richard was in love with her—except Livinia, who refused to see it, or perhaps refused to acknowledge it.

Lady Pettifer suspected she had her eyes set on someone else, someone Livinia refused to speak about, which made Lady Pettifer concerned it was some married man. As bright and gregarious as Livinia was, she did keep some things close to her chest when she wanted to.

Dory had gotten to know her much better in their time together. These days, Livinia didn't quite grate on her as much as in the beginning, but she acknowledged that they were vastly different types of people. In fact, Dory took to her role as companion very well, preferring to spend time at Ville Beaulieu with Lady Pettifer than running around the house parties in Cannes and Nice. It could also be that Dory didn't quite belong with any of the groups that milled around the coast.

In certain settings, Livinia wasn't always able to be as footloose as she wished and Dory had to serve as chaperone if any notable doyennes of etiquette from England would be there. Livinia still had her mother's scandal to contend with, so couldn't afford any tarnishing to her own reputation in certain circles.

Accepting her cup of tea, Dory held it to her mouth and drew in the scent. Lady Pettifer was very specific with her tea, and Dory had learned to tell the difference between Chinese, Indian and Ceylon teas just by the smell. It was Ceylon today.

Beauty lay panting under the table and Dory held down the last piece of her biscuit, feeling the dog's wet nose to her fingers before long.

The noisy engine of the mailman's motorcar echoed off the trees as he drove up the long, winding driveway.

"Running a bit late today," Lady Pettifer chided. "No doubt Mr. Merton was giving him trouble." Mr. Merton was their neighbor, a cantankerous elderly man who really enjoyed nothing of life, or even what the lifestyle in the south of France offered. Dory often wondered why he didn't simply be miserable back home. She'd never worked up the nerve to ask, and here on the coast, it was impolite to inquire what brought people here, because there were some who weren't strictly here by choice. Like Livinia, some fled scandal back home—or worse. For others, the temperate climate agreed with their health.

Livinia came out of the house and sat down in one of the free chairs. The music still played above in her room, almost as if she couldn't stand the silence. She checked her watch. "Where is he? He said he'd be here."

"Something must have held him up," Lady Pettifer said to assuage Livinia's annoyance. It wouldn't do that Richard was less than punctual. "I am sure that all of Cannes will not forget about you simply because you are an hour late."

Accompanying a sour look, Livinia drew a deep breath and crossed her arms. "I do wish we could build a pool. I'm sure even Dory would venture in once in a blue moon."

Lady Pettifer snorted. There is a vast sea right in front of you." Lady Pettifer couldn't abide pools. Her generation didn't build pools. It was a uniquely American import—and hence, avoided. "Besides, there is a war going on. How can we run around building swimming pools at such a time?"

"I think this war is just an excuse for not doing anything. Everyone goes on and on about this war, and nothing ever happens. I feel I have been whacked over the head with this war as far back as I can remember."

"War is simply awful," Lady Pettifer sniffed, her voice drifting off to old memories from the previous war.

Livinia didn't quite roll her eyes, but she had little tolerance for hearing about the war—this or any other.

Almost silently, Mr. Fernley appeared with a silver tray. "The mail, madam," he said in his typical dry tone. There were two letters—none for Dory. She got letters from her mother once a week, and one would likely come in the next day or so, but other than that, she had no one writing to her.

"Oh, an invitation," Livinia said, picking up an envelope of rich, creamy paper. "How exciting."

Now it was Lady Pettifer's turn to grumble as she opened her own letter and read in silence.

"A masquerade," Livinia said with excitement. "Next week. Lady Tonbridge. Well, well, that is a development, isn't it? She must be inviting everyone. That son of hers must be here. What was his name?"

"Marcus," Lady Pettifer stated.

"The invitation is for you as well."

"Not sure I have the constitution for a masquerade," Lady Pettifer said dismissively without looking up. "My knee is still giving me all sorts of trouble. Dory can go."

Automatically, Dory smiled graciously. From having been an observer of such parties back at Wallisford Hall, she was now well past any fascination she'd had for them. Her status here on the coast was not in doubt by anyone. She was never quite a part of Livinia's set, but she wasn't exactly a servant either. The fact that she had been a maid back in England was also known by quite a few. In the beginning, Livinia had pointed it out diligently. Because of this, very few people actually spoke to her at these parties she was sometimes asked to go to. "Of course," Dory said.

"It will be so much fun. It's short notice, though. I think I need a new dress. Where is Richard? I now have to run to the dressmaker as well."

In fact, Livinia's chauffeur was just arriving. They heard the sound of his car, a much deeper rumble than the high-pitched engine of the mailman. He could be heard even where they sat around the back of the house.

It didn't take him long to find them, walking around the corner of the house. "Aren't you all a picture?" he said with a broad smile. "Smart to escape the midday heat." He took a seat, pulling up the white linen material of his slacks along his long, lean legs. "There's an overturned cart on the road. Took ages to right. Silly bugger."

"I'll just get dressed," Livinia said, bounding into the house.

"I might as well get comfortable, then," Richard said with resignation.

"Tea?" Lady Pettifer offered.

"I would love a cup," he said with a smile.

Chapter 2

Most of the streets in the village of St. Tropez were too small for motor cars to get through. The alleys were tight and dark, most of the buildings three stories, rendered in oranges and yellows. Dory liked walking around here as the streets were typically quite cool, protecting the pedestrians from the heat of the sun.

It was late spring and the sun was getting stronger by the week. The heat and Lady Pettifer's knee kept her mostly at home. Over the last few months, she had increasingly been tired and feeling under the weather. The doctor said it was just a bug and nothing to worry about. Rest and relaxation was all she needed, apparently. Still, Dory couldn't help worrying.

Because of her health, though, Lady Pettifer had not felt up to returning to England for the summer. It meant staying over the hot months, but Lady Pettifer felt she preferred that to spending three weeks on a ship, plus all the trouble with making her way to Wallisford Hall again. Besides, with the war, passage wasn't as readily available as it had been.

Walking into the bakery, Dory was met with the lovely smell of fresh bread, and opened her coin purse to buy a loaf. The French were gifted with bread. Dory hadn't understood how wonderful bread could be before coming here. And the cheese. The French took their cheese as seriously as some did their whiskey.

With a smile, she paid the baker's wife and continued down to the waterfront where the fishermen were selling their morning's catch. It smelled of fish and salt, the entire village seemed to congregate down by the waterfront.

There was no sign of war here. Nothing had changed, and Dory hoped it would stay that way. Still, it felt as though they were living on borrowed time. Everyone hoped that there was sufficient deterrence on both sides to stop either from making an advance. It had kept the war from properly starting so far. God willing it held.

In saying that, anyone new in town, or even in Cannes and Nice, were treated with suspicion. Anyone of German descent had been rounded up and taken into internment—including the ones who would get no welcome in Hitler's Germany.

With carrots, fish and bread in her basket, Dory righted her bicycle and started home. Villa Beaulieu was some ways out of the village, perched on top of a cliff. It had both privacy and spectacular views, which was why Lady Pettifer had bought it with her ailing husband some time ago.

Having spent almost two years here, it was hard to consider going back to Swanley to live with her mother again. Still, Dory had to consider her future at some point, but as long as Lady Pettifer wanted her to stay, she would.

Bicycling up the hills made sweat run down her back and she had to get off and push. This was a route Dory cycled every day, and still, it made her smile every time she looked out at the sea. Small boats sat in the distance, the blue of the sea having turned hazy in the afternoon.

Dory was puffed by the time she made it home and walked into the cool interior of Villa Beaulieu, to find Lady Pettifer sitting in the salon by the large open window. Italian paintings hung on the walls and the sumptuous articles of furniture were all older than Dory was. It was a house where everything had its proper place and little had changed or moved since the time the house had been set up. From what she suspected, the penchant for Italian furniture had been Lady Pettifer's husband, but since his death, she hadn't changed a thing.

The Pettifers hadn't built the house, though. It had been some acquaintance they'd known, an older couple that had passed away quite some while ago.

"The mailman came while you were away. There is a letter from your mother."

"Oh," Dory said and sat down, seeing the letter waiting for her. It had a large sticking along the edge of the envelope that said, 'Opened by the Censor.' Dory opened it. It was strange to think someone had read her correspondence with her mother, but there was nothing for it. it was simply a part of life, these days.

The letter contained nothing but her mother's musings and her ongoing concerns for Dory's siblings. As it was, Dory sent most of her salary back home, so everyone was fed and thriving—but that didn't stop her mother from worrying.

"No news of Margot and her baby?" Lady Pettifer asked, who was by now well-versed in the goings ons amongst the members of the Sparks family. Margot was Dory's cousin and was expecting a baby any day.

"She doesn't say, so I'm guessing she hasn't had it yet. I think it will be a boy, though. I just get that feeling."

"A letter came from Vivian," Lady Pettifer said.

"Oh." Dory felt her shoulders stiffen. She'd heard very little from or about Vivian since they had left England. Her relationship with Vivian, Lady Pettifer's nephew and Livinia's twin, had always been tentative and uncomfortable.

"He says he's in Geneva."

A second rush of discomfort washed over her. His mother, the murderess of Nora Sands, was currently institutionalized in a Swiss sanitorium, and that could be the only reason he would be there.

"I think there is a strong possibility he'll come for a visit, but he doesn't say what his plans are. Only that Honoria is fine and it's a lovely place."

A tight smile twisted Dory's lips. In a sense, Lady Wallisford had gotten away with murder, being subsequently placed in a sanatorium. Technically, she wasn't free to leave, but it was better than she deserved. A young woman was dead for that woman's over eagerness to protect her childrens' ambitions. The whole affair turned Dory's stomach.

"It is still a prison," Lady Pettifer said as if reading Dory's thoughts. They remained silent for a while. The tentacles of that dastardly deed still reached far and wide. "Never mind. It's quite exciting about the masquerade."

Dory nodded, appreciative of the change in subject.

"I'm glad you're getting out and about a bit. You shouldn't be stuck here with an old woman all the time."

"I am a companion. This is exactly what I am supposed to do." This was an ongoing discussion between them, and in a sense, Dory was hiding from life a little in this comfortable house. Not that she minded. This had been a place of discovery. She had learned so much during her time here—things she would never have experienced back in Swanley. Lady Pettifer was concerned because she didn't spend copious amounts of time with people her own age, like Livinia did, but Dory's concern was more that her life was a little too easy here. She literally had nothing to worry about other than Lady Pettifer's health.

"I am sure it will be a very diverting party. Livinia seems excited," Dory said brightly.

"Livinia would be excited about a queue at the post office if it had the right dress code."

Dory chuckled. Sadly, it was true. Livinia treasured anyone's company but her own.

But Dory couldn't stop thinking that she should be more like Livinia and seek the company of others. Obviously, Livinia's set wouldn't be welcoming, but surely there would be people in the area who would welcome her as a friend. It just seemed such a hassle to go all the way to Cannes to seek them out.

*

Supper was eaten by candlelight. An officer from the French territorial army had come around a few months back and insisted they stay dark at night. Lady Pettifer had been deeply offended by his tone, but had grudgingly acknowledged the need for it. No one wanted Germans flying around with their bombers at night, did they?

The arrival of German planes had never happened, but that did not provide the excuse for being lax. Granted, many were. Some people along the coast failed to understand the concept of a blackout, and at times, the authorities had to resort to cutting the power.

The cook was an elderly French woman, who created the most divine meals. Lady Pettifer had running battles with the woman who preferred the heavy French palate with thick sauces, scoops of butter and cream. It didn't agree with Lady Pettifer's digestion, but cook had her strict view of what made a decent meal. Gladys, Dory's aunt, would likely be offended by the woman and the meals she served, but Dory could never complain. The French food was marvelous—although, at times, she had to take an extra hour to walk it off.

"Sherry, dear?" Lady Pettifer asked and Mr. Fernley prepared the salon for them.

"A small one would be nice." Dory didn't know how she would live as an elderly lady, but she would never complain with a setup like this. In saying that, though, as time passed and the scandal of Lady Wallisford's activities died down, there would be a time when Dory really should return to England and find a place for herself—unless this war started in earnest and took all choices out of her hands.

The truth was that Dory had no idea what war entailed. Lady Pettifer had once said that the women of England, and broader Britain as well, would have to take over the ongoing operation of the country. It seemed an extraordinary notion, but Dory had to concede that she was probably right. Dory just didn't have a good understanding of how that would work.

DI Ridley entered her mind and she wondered if the Police would need women as well. Could Dory ever consider a profession in the Police? She wasn't sure if she could do what he did. Her eagerness to solve a crime had been a bit of a revelation and she was still deeply offended by someone getting away with an action as awful as taking someone's life.

"Mr. Fernley, would you be so kind to turn the wireless on." Lady Pettifer asked as she settled herself. "Let's hear what they have to say tonight."

The radio started with a rush of static before Mr. Fernley corrected the setting. Music played for a little while and Beauty settled herself down to lie by Lady Pettifer's feet.

It went quiet for a moment, followed by a series of familiar beeps. Everyone in the room was utterly still.

This is the BBC in London calling, the man started with his sharp, deep tone. We start tonight's bulletin with news regarding Germany's advancement into Denmark and Norway, which commenced this morning in the early hours of dawn.

Dory shuddered at what she heard and they all exchanged worried glances.

"It seems they are taking over anywhere they can get a foothold," Lady Pettifer said.

"At least they cannot breach the French Army," Dory said quietly.

"Let's hope that deters them. I do hope Vivian is safe in Switzerland."

Dory noted that she didn't extend the concern to Lady Wallisford, which showed how low a regard she truly had for the woman. At least they agreed on that.

The man broadcasting went on to say the German Army had landed by sea at Gedser and were moving north, and that German troops had sailed up the Oslofjord to the capital of Norway.

Every moment seemed to make it all sound worse. Germans simply invading. It was worse than Dory could imagine. Those horrid Nazis and their relentless ambition. There was no talk of appeasement anymore. They were at war, but opposing sides of equal might deterred any real fighting.

Chapter 3

"I have sent Mr. Fernley up in the attic to find my old mask. I bought it in Venice a while ago now, and it will serve you well for the evening," Lady Pettifer said as Dory sat in the salon and read.

"That's wonderful. I had figured I would have to fashion myself something out of the material from an old hat."

"We can do better than that."

Livina's dress had been delivered that afternoon in a large, paper box and Livinia was already upstairs, the dulcet tone of her music playing as it always did.

"If it proves to be too difficult to drive back at night, you can always stay with Lady Dorsey. She wouldn't mind one bit."

Dory had been worried about driving the road back in the dark. It all depended on how bright the moon was. If there was no moon, it was an uncomfortable and perilous journey with steep drops and sharp turns. The coastline undulated violently between St. Tropez and Cannes. "Hopefully, we will make it back."

Another concern was that Livinia would go off with her friends and simply leave Dory to her own devices. Well, perhaps not a concern so much as a real possibility. Livinia was always willing to keep the party going. Dory, on the other hand, was not willing to follow some group around in the wee hours of the night. That would be too much. If Livinia refused to come home, Dory was not prepared to take any responsibility for that—and Lady Pettifer wouldn't expect her to. Livinia was technically old enough to make her own decisions.

In a sense, Dory had some sympathy for Livinia, who was expected to straddle two different social expectations—the old, where she was supposed to be a demure innocent, protected from the world and any real role in it, and also the expectations of a modern girl who made her own way in the world. She needed to be both things at once, and she was managing—perhaps embracing the modern girl a little too gleefully, but that was simply Dory's opinion.

"Have you been successful?" Lady Pettifer asked as Mr. Fernley returned with a box.

"Is this the one you were referring to?" he said, opening the box.

Inside was a white mask with feathers and gold trimming. It looked like a sugar confection, much too fancy, but it was better than any monstrosity that Dory could create, so in that regard, Dory was pleased.

"I think this will go better with your blue dress," Lady Pettifer said.

Dory had two fancy dresses that she used for parties and events. She loved both of them, but she couldn't say she felt entirely comfortable in them. Those dresses were the embodiment of the discomfort she felt about how she fit in here. The truth was that living here and living this lifestyle had changed her in both outlook and in the things she wanted. Or perhaps it was more that she didn't exactly know what she wanted anymore.

"I better go change," Dory said, taking the beautifully embellished mask that Mr. Fernley had found in the treasure trove that was Lady Pettifer's attic. The material was silk, which felt buttery under her fingers. It had a dreamy quality to it and Dory wondered if she'd feel dreamy wearing it. Maybe a masquerade was something a bit special, a place where she could step outside of herself for a little while.

Changing quickly, she pulled the mask over her eyes and considered herself in the mirror. Didn't she look mysterious. Perhaps she would meet a mysterious man and they would dance, the whole while never knowing each other's identities. With a sigh, she pulled it off again and made her way downstairs.

It didn't take long for Livinia to appear, looking wonderful in a sleeveless peach dress. The dressmaker in Cannes was gifted, Dory had to concede. It was a dress far above her own, but Dory wasn't sure she would even feel comfortable in a dress like that. Livinia had no limitations to what she felt comfortable wearing.

"Ready to go?" Livinia asked, pulling up her long, satin gloves. "I'll drive." Which meant it would be an uncomfortable ride for Dory as Livinia's rash behavior was evident in her driving too. The whole family had issues with driving, it seemed. Perhaps it was hereditary.

Dory nodded and Lady Pettifer bid them goodbye, standing at the door to see them off. Lady Pettifer's car was a burgundy-colored Bentley and as it was a dry evening, Mr. Fernley had put the canvas roof down for them.

"Well, I hope the old girl doesn't have too dull a night without us," Livinia stated. "It's so awful with her knee. It must be dreadful getting old."

"Yes," Dory had to agree.

"Andrew should come visit more often. He never comes. Finds it too hot. Such an Englishmen. Positively wilts in the heat. I, on the other hand, adore it. Who wants to molder away in the country all summer?"

More than a few times, Dory had wondered if Livinia told herself so because she was frightened to go home, frightened of the scandal her mother still was. As bright and shiny as Livinia was, she couldn't escape being tarred with that brush. But she had found both excitement and acceptance here on the coast, so Dory expected she would stay here forever if she could—at least until no one cared about the Wallisford Hall murder.

Everyone had their problems, even someone as lofty and flighty as Livinia.

The sky was painted in all shades of orange, red and mauve. It was utterly beautiful and the air was fresh as they drove. Dusk was quickly settling and Dory hoped they would get to their destination before dark. Livinia certainly seemed to be in a hurry to get there.

They drove in silence, because as usually was, they had precious little to talk about, but knew each other enough to sit in silence. Dory had no illusions about what Livinia thought of her—boring and pointless. She was never mean about it. Meanness wasn't actually part of Livinia's personality. Only her brothers brought that out in her.

"You look nice," Livinia finally said.

"Thank you," Dory replied.

"I think your mask is actually better than mine. Who knew Aunt Connie had that up in the attic?"

For a moment, Dory wondered if Livinia wanted it, but she didn't say so. Hopefully not, because Livinia's mask would clash horribly with Dory's dress. "I wonder if the Duke and Duchess will be there," she said instead, referring to the notorious Windsors.

"They might. I suspect they would love to come to a masquerade and not be noticed. Everyone continually stares at them otherwise." Dory had seen them once at one of the well-known annual parties held by someone with a hyphenated name ending with Rothchild. The ambitious approached them, but mostly, people simply observed them. "I don't think I could stand that."

"You hate being noticed in any capacity," Livinia pointed out. It was hard to argue, but Dory was surprised that Livinia had even noticed that about her.

"That training to never be seen is hard to shake," she said by way of defending herself.

Livinia gave her a chiding glance. "Can't blame your shyness on training."

Dory utterly hated discussing herself and her shortcomings. At least Livinia knew exactly what she wanted in life. She wanted to marry well, with a handsome, rich man who also wanted to be the life of the party. The only ambition Dory had managed to muster was to perhaps go to secretarial school, and even that didn't set her heart alight.

"I'm not planning on coming home tonight," Livinia said after a while. "Duckie is having a party at his house tomorrow, so I thought I'd stay. You don't mind driving back on your own, do you?"

"No, of course not." She didn't relish driving back in the dark, but that had nothing to do with having Livinia's company.

"It's going to be a smashing night. I understand they are having a performance by some American jazz singer."

"You wouldn't know there was a war on, would you?"

"The Germans can keep their war. Miserable buggars. I hope they choke on it."

Dory smiled. There was no holding back with Livinia; she charged ahead with whatever opinion she had.

"Did Lady Pettifer tell you she got a letter from Vivian?"

By Livinia's raised eyebrows, Dory had her answer. "Is that so?"

"He's in Switzerland, it seems."

Livinia's expression clouded over. She wasn't remotely as forgiving of their mother as Vivian seemed to be. It was a hard thing to accept, perhaps.

"Here we are," Livinia said and took an exit off the road. A house was lit up like a firecracker up the side of the hill. It was just about completely dark now and there was no one in doubt there was a party going on. Any German flying over would see a glowing point on an otherwise—mostly—dark coastline.

Chapter 4

The house itself was large, looming over the dark mountainside like a crouching cat. The moon was almost full, so the outline of the hill and the house was seen, as well as the sea beyond. It was a beautiful place, giving Dory the feel of isolation, as though it was an oceangoing ship. Cars were parked along the driveway and Livinia squeezed into a spot with barely enough room to get out.

"Come on," she said excitedly as they walked the rest of the way up to the house. Music was heard even from here, and live music, not the sedate scratchy tunes from a gramophone. Livinia busied herself with her mask and Dory followed. It felt a little suffocating having something on her face, but that was all a part of it.

A neatly dressed servant stood in the doorway with a tray of champagne and Livinia sailed past, picking one up on the way. She really was in her element.

"Thank you," Dory said as she grabbed a glass. Champagne was marvelous and the French really had a way of making the humble grape into something magical.

Meeting her was a room full of exquisitely dressed people, all wearing masks—some elaborate, some plain black. The men all wore black tails with neatly combed hair. This was Livinia's crowd and they was glittering. There was more jewelry in this room than Dory knew how to take in. This wasn't her first event, but this might be the most stylish.

There were some older attendees as well. Their style was slightly different, older in fashion, but there was still a sense of waylaid inhibitions. Obviously, she had heard them exalt what the Cote d'Azur was like in the twenties, with the lavish parties. These days, things were more sedate to reflect the times, and the fact that the country was at war—but not tonight. Tonight was an unapologetic return to opulence.

In a way, Dory was glad she was here. Few of her friends back in Swanley would ever believe there were parties like this. It was too much for the senses to take in.

On a table across the room, a champagne pyramid stood, and a man poured into the very top glass until it overflowed to all the glasses below. There was also an ice sculpture of a crane with its neck looped around as if it were surveying its own leg.

A girl in a red, tasseled top and small shorts walked around with a silver ice bucket. "For the war effort," she said expectantly as she waited for a man to consult his wallet. In the end, the task proved too difficult so he dropped the whole wallet in. "Good man," she said with a broad smile and moved to the next.

Dory only had five francs in her small purse, but she supposed she would have to part with it when the girl came her way. Everyone needed to do their bit for the war, although she hadn't expected it to be a part of a night like this.

The inside of the main reception room had tall palm trees in pots. The fronds curved across the people milling. Sleek art graced the walls. It really was a lovely house. The floor was black and white checkered, which showed that this house was probably built ten years ago. It was a house built to dazzle and it did its job in that regard. Ville Beaulieu was much older with its cream stucco walls, wood and terracotta floors. As stylish as this house was, Dory preferred the comfort of Beaulieu.

Walking along, Dory smiled to anyone who smiled at her. She was enjoying just seeing this party and the people here. A dance floor was filled with milling couples—some obviously in love. Livinia was one of the dancers, who was laughing at something said by a tall man with glossy black hair. Was this the man she seemed so eager to see, the one she didn't really speak about?

It wasn't Duckie. Dory had met Duckie before, so she knew Livinia was dancing with someone else. It could be that he was the reason she was staying behind tonight—not that Livinia needed a reason. Dory hoped she knew what she was doing.

But then who was she to judge? When it came to love, she wasn't exactly thriving in that department. Back home, she'd never really had time for boys, and it wasn't until she'd met DI Ridley that she'd even managed a proper blush. It was impossible not to face the fact that she had been sweet on him, and to her eternal gratitude, he hadn't noticed. That was all said and done now.

Perhaps part of the reason she stayed on here in the South of France, besides the obvious comfort of her life here, was that she didn't want to go back to England, where she would naturally go to London, to then discover that DI

Ridley had absolutely no interest in her now that his case was solved. Part of her obviously feared that was true.

The fact still was that while she had blushed whenever he'd shown a modicum of concern for her wellbeing, he hadn't blushed back. He wasn't the kind of man to blush. With him, he had his objective in mind, and probably didn't notice anything unrelated—like blushing maids.

Changing direction, Dory tried to put all that out of her mind. What she really needed was a seat somewhere, where she could perch for a while like any self-respecting wallflower.

"Hello, Dory," a man said and Dory turned to see Duckie.

"I see my attempts at going incognito have completely failed. What gave me away?" Probably the dress as she only had two to wear. Surely he must have noticed.

Duckie smiled, his eyes looking disturbingly disembodied behind the mask. "Not sure. I think it's the hair. Since you are here, I assume Livinia is milling around."

"Last I saw her, she was on the dance floor." For officially being a chaperone, that sounded awful, but to be fair, she was expected to be the semblance of a chaperone rather than an active one.

A sharp scream echoed across the room, enough to make Dory drop her glass, which smashed into a thousand pieces around her feet. That wasn't the scream of some drunk girl being tickled. There was terror in that scream. Were the Germans invading, was the first thought that stole through Dory's brain.

Duckie's hand was on her arm as if steadying her. The music stopped and confusion spread through the crowd like a malignancy. Then murmurs. Everyone turned and stared in the direction of the scream.

A man cleared his throat. "I think we shall require the service of the Police. There has been an incident."

Livinia pressed unseeingly through the crowd, tears flowing down her face. Dory grabbed her by the arms to stop her. "What happened?"

"I don't know. I went to the bathroom and when I came back... he was dead."

"Who?" Duckie asked avidly.

"Drecsay," Livinia said, distress clearly showing in her eyes. "There was blood." At this moment, she looked like a small child who had been chastised for the first time. "He's dead."

"Bollocks," Duckie said.

People started leaving, finding a place to put their glasses down and headed to the door. Cars were already roaring to life outside, as they made their escape.

"We should go," Duckie said. "Where's Margot?"

"You can't go," Dory said, still holding onto Livinia by the arms as if she'd escape the moment she let go. "You found the body, you need to stay."

Livinia's expression turned to full-on pouting. "I can't."

"You have to. You found the body," Dory repeated.

"I didn't murder him."

"So don't make it look like it by scarpering."

To her credit, Livinia seemed to accept this, but with that acceptance, she now looked faint, as if the shock was catching up with her. Duckie came to her aid and they walked over to a seat.

A few people were still milling about, but from the window, Dory could see a string of car headlights making their way down the mountainside like a sparkling necklace in the darkness.

Couples stood near each other with their arms wrapped around them. A man who had to be the resident butler was trying to take control, and he was flustered, completely unsure what to do.

"Did you call the police?" Dory asked.

The man nodded. "I called them and they said they'd be here in ten minutes."

"Right," Dory said. It was clear where the body was. Down a hallway, a crowd had gathered, all staring down. "We need to clear the area."

The butler still looked confused, too flustered to do anything useful, so Dory walked over to where the crowd was.

"We should probably let the police do their job," she said. "Perhaps we should close the doors until they get here." A couple of people were staring absently at her, as if they didn't understand what she was saying. "Which means you should leave now," she said in a harsher voice. The terseness seemed to motivate the people to move. A voice of authority got through even if it came from her. "Off you go," she continued, eyeing everyone who hadn't gotten the message, until they all left.

A man was crouched next to the body. "You, too," she said and the man eyed her with offense for a moment, before acknowledging that she was right.

The dead man lay on his back, his eyes staring at the ceiling. It was such an unnatural look that goosebumps crawled up Dory's skin. There was clearly blood on the side of his head, and it was the man she had seen Livinia dancing with before, except his mask wasn't on. He was clearly a handsome man, even in death.

Refusing to look more, she grabbed the edges of the double doors and closed what looked like a study. Now, like everyone else, she didn't know what to do with herself. It felt wrong shutting him away to be there alone and discarded. Everything about this felt wrong. It was wrong. A man had lost his life, and by the look of his wound, it hadn't been an accident. He'd been murdered mere yards away from the party.

Chapter 5

The house stood in utter silence while they waited for the police. Another couple decided it was time to go and quietly slipped away. In rushed voices, they spoke to the butler as they left, then their car was clearly heard as they backed up before rushing down the driveway.

Livinia was sitting against the wall, leaning against Duckie's shoulder, while Dory stood in the center of the room, unsure what else to do. One man—clearly drunk—was pouring himself another generous portion of champagne from a discarded bottle.

No one spoke again and from somewhere, Dory heard the ticking of a clock.

How long was it going to take for the police to arrive?

Eventually a car snaked up the side of the mountain and Dory felt relief, as if release from this awkwardness was pending.

Car doors slammed outside and then a man appeared, marching straight into the room in a beige uniform with a pistol holstered at his side, secured with a leather strap crossed his chest. He wore a bored and unhappy expression, showing that he really didn't want to deal with hysterical Brits and their problems.

His gaze traveled across the room, noting the people there. Again, the butler assumed that it was his role to try to deal with this, but the inspector dismissed him with a terse look and the butler visibly deflated.

In the exchange, the inspector had learned where the problem was and walked over to the hallway that led to the study. He opened the doors and stepped inside.

Another policeman stood at the main doors, eyeing them all suspiciously. Everyone else shifted uncomfortably, feeling like naughty school children about to be told off.

Richard appeared, wearing his black tails and holding a small sandwich in his hand. His eyes shifted to Livinia sitting with Duckie and then further, finding Dory. Instead of joining Livinia, he decided to join Dory.

"I hadn't realized you were here," Dory said.

"I came late. Missed the party, but caught the main event."

Dory didn't like how casually he said it.

"Do you think someone snuck in the window and killed him?" he asked.

With a snort, Dory looked away. "The window was closed." In her experience, it was rarely strangers that snuck in and performed some horrid misdeed, even though it was what people liked to assume. No one automatically thought that someone among their friends and acquaintances was a murderer.

"Seems like a dire sort of chap, doesn't he?"

"Drecsay?" Dory asked, recalling the name Livinia had used. Dory had never seen him before tonight, or noticed him if she had.

"No, the policeman."

"Technically, I believe he's a gendarmerie instead of a policeman, but either way, he isn't here to make friends," Dory said dismissively. "He needs to suspect everyone."

"Ohh, I've never been a suspect before. Have you?"

"No," Dory admitted.

"Nothing to put a dampener on a party like a murder," Richard chuckled. "Poor Elsbeth. She had such high hopes for this party. Well, it truly will be the most notorious party of the season. Not quite how she anticipated, no doubt."

"Did you know the man?"

"Drecsay? I suppose. Everyone knows Drecsay. Been around for ages. Handsome bugger. Ladies like him." Richard took a bite of his sandwich and chewed. Well, he was certainly not one to faint with shock. In fact, he seemed completely unperturbed by the events. "I don't suppose we can leave."

"By the look of the man at the door, I don't think any of us are leaving until they've done what they want."

Richard checked his wrist watch.

"Somewhere you need to be?"

"No, not particularly."

"Who was he, this Drecsay?"

"Well," Richard started as if he was about to embark on a rambling story. "Hungarian baron from what I understand—if you believe what he said, because you never know about some of these foreign aristocrats, do you? Poor as a church mouse. You know the type, likes to mingle where the rich ladies are. Flatters them with charm and compliments. They lap it up, of course. The place is filthy with them. He has some rooms at one of the hotels in Nice, I believe."

And that had been who Livinia had been dancing with. Is that what he'd done to Livinia, charmed her? She was, after all, a wealthy heiress. If this man was the type that Richard painted, then he could well have been seeking an improvement in his position through the association. Dory sighed. Surely Livinia wasn't stupid enough to fall for such a man, was she? At times Dory felt like the ugly stepsister to Cinderella, provided Cinderella was resoundingly vacant and a bit of an idiot, chasing after some wildly inappropriate prince. Technically, it was Lady Pettifer's job to keep Livinia out of trouble, but it was Dory's too by extension.

The policeman appeared. "And who is this man?" he said with a flourish of his hand toward the study.

The butler stepped forward. "His name is Baron Dominik Drecsay. I am sure he has a string of middle names, but I do not know them."

The inspector turned to the butler without expression, then nodded to the policeman by the door, who promptly scribbled it down in his notebook.

"And everyone who was here at the time has left," the inspector continued.

"Yes," said the butler with a blush. "Mostly." Now a blushing butler was a rare sight in Dory's book, but then there had been admonishment in the inspector's statement.

"Who discovered the body?"

Everyone turned to Livinia, who still clung to Duckie for support. With raised eyebrows, the inspector walked over. Livinia looked up at him with large, wounded eyes. Dory had to stop herself from rolling hers.

"Who are you, and what were the circumstances in which you found him?"

"Well," Livinia said. "I am Livinia Fellingworth, daughter of Lord Wallisford. I had been in the bathroom and I was walking past."

"But the bathroom is nowhere near the study."

The wounded expression fleeted from Livinia's eyes. She didn't like being challenged, and she certainly didn't like admitting that she had been seeking out the company of Baron Drecsay in the isolation of the study. It wasn't seemly.

"Like I said," she said in a sterner voice. "I was walking past and he was simply lying there. Bloody."

"And the door was open?"

"A little."

The inspector looked down his nose at her. Clearly, the man didn't believe her story, or at least the embellishments.

"And this man was your lover?"

"What? No!" Livinia said with deep offense.

"He is a handsome man. It is understandable if you were sneaking off for a rendezvous in a more private place."

"Absolutely not," Livina said sternly, but she was unable to hide the blush on her cheeks.

"And before you found him in the library? Where did you see him?"

Livinia's mouth drew tight. "On the dance floor."

"You were dancing, yes?"

"Yes," Livinia said through gritted teeth.

The inspector was eyeing her now and Dory knew he was wondering if she had murdered him in some jealous tiff. Absolutely not, Dory thought. For all of Livinia's shortcomings, she didn't feel any emotion deeply enough to drive her to murder.

"I didn't really know him," Livinia filled in as the silence stretched. "The evening has been quite a shock. Can we go now?"

"And where do you live, Mademoiselle Fellingworth?" Her name sounded like an insult in the French accent. Dory wasn't sure if it was intended that way or not.

"Saint Tropez. Ville Beaulieu."

A short grunt escaped the inspector. Seemingly, he wasn't pleased with this. Probably because it was quite some way from this man's office, which Dory guessed was in Cannes.

Then he turned his attention to the rest of the people present, asking who they were, where they had been during the party and the discovery, how they knew the deceased and where they lived. Also if they knew of any enemies the man had. After, they could all go home.

Dory could hear the man request the guest list for the party. He had a big task ahead of him, because it had been large, and someone at the party had murdered this man. The thought made her shudder—someone stalking around the house with such ill intent.

The air was cool as they walked out of the house. Dory had no idea what time it was, but it was late.

"Are you coming home, Livinia?" Dory asked as they stood outside in the darkness. It was too dark to see Livinia's facial expressions. Her whole face had a blue quality from the moonlight.

"I think I will, actually," she said to Dory's surprise. It seemed there was something that could quell her social yearnings.

"Alright, let's go," Dory said and they found their car, which had been standing on its own as everyone else had left. Now there was sufficient space to maneuver as they got in and turned around to leave. The engine whined on the way down the hill and luckily, the moonlight was enough to see the road beyond the short reach of the headlights.

Quiet contemplation seemed to be Livinia's current disposition. It had been quite a shocking night for her, Dory supposed.

"Were you in love with this man?" Dory asked after a while.

"No, of course not," Livinia replied. Her voice sounded thin and distant, so Dory wasn't sure whether she was telling the truth or not.

It hit Dory how incredible this all was. A man had been murdered right there when they were all chatting and drinking champagne. How in the world could something like that happen?

"Do you have any idea who killed him?" Dory asked.

"What I said was true. I didn't really know him that well. I didn't know of any enemies as such. He was just someone around, you know? No one particularly hated him; he was a charming man."

Charming didn't automatically mean no one hated him, but Dory wasn't sure it was the time to point that out.

Chapter 6

Dory was exhausted the next day. Sleep had eluded her and her mind had repeatedly turned over every detail from the night before. And still, she couldn't believe someone had murdered that poor man. He couldn't be more than thirty. His whole life was ahead of him and it had been snuffed out—for apparently no reason at all.

There was a reason, though. No one was bludgeoned at a party for absolutely no reason. Someone hated this man enough to kill him. Then again, murder wasn't always about hate. Lady Wallisford hadn't hated when she'd killed. In her mind, she'd been protecting her family. Murder could be cold and calculating.

Turning herself over, Dory tried fruitlessly to fall off to sleep, but the sun was up and the birds were chirping. Perhaps it was time to give up and embrace a day of sluggish exhaustion. With heavy legs, she dragged herself out of bed and dressed. Dark shadows were pronounced under her eyes. Brilliant. She looked like a train wreck.

The house was mostly quiet when she went downstairs, although she could hear the tinkling of cutlery. Lady Pettifer was up and breakfasting when Dory walked into the dining room.

"My dear," Lady Pettifer said. "By the look of you, it must have been a long night."

"Not in the way you think. There was an incident at the party which ended it early. A man—someone Livinia knows, and was dancing with, in fact—ended up bludgeoned in the study."

Deep concern marred Lady Pettifer's face. "I hope he's alright."

Dory shook her head, hating that she had to be the one relaying these events.

"Who?" Lady Pettifer demanded.

"Some Baron Drecsay, a Hungarian."

"I don't know him."

"I don't either, but Livinia does—did—and according to Richard, he might not be the type of man she should be spending time with."

"Not if he runs around being murdered. How awful." Lady Pettifer shuddered and Beauty jumped up into her lap. "I suppose the police will let the Hungarian ambassador know."

"That seems logical."

They sat in silence for a moment, and Mr. Fernley placed down a plate of eggs and toast in front of Dory. "Thank you," she mumbled, completely unable to gather her appetite, but she ate to be agreeable. "I am sure the inspector will come around and question Livinia more at some point."

Picking up her coffee cup, Lady Pettifer absently drank and returned it. "What sort of man was he?"

"Well, according to Richard, he was poor and maybe even dependent on the more wealthy ladies of the area."

Lady Pettifer winced. "Still, that doesn't really lend itself to murder, does it? Who would kill a man like that?"

Someone like Lady Wallisford, Dory thought, chewing her toast and looking away. "Maybe he had garnered the attention of some woman and her family objected."

"Hardly cause for murder," Lady Pettifer said. "Then again, people murder for all sorts of reasons, don't they? I don't like that Livinia is caught up in all this."

"No," Dory agreed. With her own eyes, she had already seen that inspector consider whether Livinia was the murderer. There was a good chance he would continue with that line of questioning.

"Bludgeoned, you said?" Lady Pettifer asked after a while. "That most certainly has to be a man. I'm not sure a women could bludgeon a man to death." Dory wasn't sure if that was true, but she wasn't an expert.

"I didn't get a close look, but I don't think he was hit repeatedly. At least not from what I could see. There could have been injuries that I couldn't see. I didn't get a chance to study him. There was a marble clock nearby him on the floor, and I am almost certain that was the weapon."

"Anyone could have walked in, whacked him on the head, and slipped out again. How many people were at this party?"

"It seemed like two hundred."

She winced and a silence prevailed again. It was utterly silent upstairs, too. No music was playing, so Livinia was asleep.

"Had Livinia been carrying on with this man?" Lady Pettifer asked.

Dory could only shrug. "I hope not. They had been dancing together, and—she says otherwise—but she was meeting him in the study, where she found him dead."

"Poor Livinia. She must be distraught. She wasn't built for such knocks. Too high-strung."

As if awakened by people speaking about her, the music started playing upstairs.

"It seems she's awake," Lady Pettifer said. "I hope she isn't too distraught. I haven't heard her mention this man before, so who can say what kind of relationship she had with him."

Livinia eventually appeared down on the patio wearing sunglasses. Her hair had been quickly brushed and she wore a white shirt and shorts. For the terrible night, she looked fresh. "God, I'm parched," she said and sat down. She reached for the jug of orange juice and poured herself a helping.

"I'm sorry to hear about the dreadful events last night."

Livinia shrugged her shoulders. "I can't make heads or tails of it. Who could possibly hate Drecsay enough to do that to him? You don't suppose it was an accident?"

"No," Dory said with certainty. It wasn't that he lay close to the fireplace to suggest he could have accidentally fallen and dragged the clock down upon himself. No, someone had picked up the clock and smashed him over the head with it. In fact, the person had probably been watching Drecsay in the main salon, then watched for an opportunity to strike when Livinia was absent. That had to mean that the person was watching Livinia dance with the man during the evening. The thought made Dory uncomfortable and the hairs rose along her arms. Had the person planned what to do? Had they come to the party with the intention of murdering someone?

"It's such a shame," Livinia sighed wistfully. "He was such a gorgeous man. Do you think someone killed him because they were jealous?"

"Not sure people go around murdering others simply because they're pretty," Lady Pettifer said.

"There's a mercy," Livinia responded.

"But people certainly do murder because of jealousy."

"That seems pointless. If there is something you want badly enough, just go out and get it."

"I think often, my dear, there is more a desire for the other person not to have what they have."

"I don't understand it at all," Livinia said dismissively, as though she didn't wish to speak about it further.

"So what do you know about this man?" Lady Pettifer asked.

Livinia sighed audibly. "Well, he's young and handsome. Lives in the Carlone on the Promenade de Anglais as far as I know. I haven't been there if that's what you're thinking," she said defensively. "He was just a nice, charming man. I can't believe someone murdered him." Her mouth was drawn tight for a moment.

"Was there anyone he'd had discord with lately?" Dory asked.

"No. There was a woman he was very close to, a Countess Tirau, but she died recently. Treated him like a son. Obviously, he wasn't a saint. There were more than a few girls vying for his attention, I'm sure. Some of the American girls used to fall over themselves when he came around. It was tiresome, really. Handsome, swarthy baron; they were beside themselves."

Reaching into her pocket, Livinia pulled out a packet of cigarettes and lit one with a gold plated lighter. She blew the smoke across the table and rested her hand to the side until the smoke from the burning tip curled up into the air.

"And where was he from?" Lady Pettifer asked.

"Hungary."

"But where in Hungary?"

"Well, I don't know, do I? Why would I ask that? It wasn't as if I made a detailed study of his family history. His family was old and respected. Ask anyone."

Livinia got up and walked away, having had enough of the questioning. Although she had better get used to it; there were likely more questions to come. The acrid smoke stung Dory's nose as she walked past.

"She is upset," Lady Pettifer stated.

In her jarring and rather dismissive way, Livinia was more upset than she let on. "Everyone on the coast must be talking about her in relation to this murder. She was the one he was meeting in the study."

"The last thing Livinia needs is another scandal."

Well, there might just be one. There would be speculation about who had killed him and why, and

Livinia's name would be in the thick of it. Problem was, with a man like Drecsay, who knew what skeletons and misdeeds he had in his closet. From what Richard said, he wasn't an innocent. Even Livinia confirmed it. But Livinia was clearly confused about why he would be murdered, so either she didn't know him well, or he really hadn't done anything that would warrant such a deplorable fate.

Chapter 7

They had a couple of quiet days at the house—days that were constantly accompanied with Livinia's gramophone. Fortunately, she had very good taste in music, so no one minded the dulcet tones of Bing Crosby and Duke Ellington. They even lent a joviality that wouldn't exist otherwise. The death of Baron Drecsay sat like a cloying heaviness, even though neither Dory nor Lady Pettifer knew him. It was the fact that it had happened that was disturbing.

The coast was such a safe community, where everyone was respected and showed a duty of care in return. Normally, the biggest problem around here were motorcar accidents, which happened relatively often late at night after some raucous party.

Dory bicycled down to the village and back, taking Beauty with her. She resupplied them with fresh bread and even bought some lemons to squeeze into drinks during the afternoon heat. Fortunately, they had enough sugar, but she had noticed that the packets of sugar in the shop were fewer than normal. Everything else seemed fine. It was just the sugar that was low. Perhaps it was just an anomaly.

"They had barely any sugar in the village store," Dory said when she returned to the house and found Lady Pettifer sitting in the parlor. She preferred it in there when the midday heat became too strong as the solid walls of the house kept the inside relatively cool.

Lady Pettifer looked up from her book. "I hope they haven't started rationing. We might see less and less of anything coming across the Atlantic."

Dory listened with concern. She hadn't realized that there might be trouble with sugar coming across from South America.

"In 1917, the Germans decided to starve us by sinking any ship coming by water."

"They said on the wireless that the navy was protecting the supply across the Atlantic," Dory said with a deep frown, trying to understand what this all meant.

"France doesn't have the same naval capabilities, so they can't provide the same degree of protection." Lady Pettifer sighed and stroked her fingers across her lips. "Mr. Fernley," she called.

He appeared mere moments later. "Can I be of assistance, Madame?"

"I think we should shore up our stores. Would you go to Cannes and purchase enough of the essentials to last us a good while? Dory has noticed things becoming scarcer down in the village."

Mr. Fernley nodded. He was old enough to remember how things had been in the first war. For all Dory knew, he might have fought in the first war. It had never occurred to her to ask him. "Yes, madame," he said. "If you shall have no use for the motorcar this afternoon, I will go presently."

"We have no plans," Lady Pettifer said and returned to her book.

He didn't wait long and Dory soon heard the car start up and caught glimpse of him drive along the trees in the distance until he was out of sight. It hadn't occurred to Dory that there would be rationing. Of course she had heard of it. Gladys had mentioned it a few times, talked about the things they'd had to do to compensate, but Dory hadn't really paid attention. It seemed vitally important now. What if they didn't have food?

"How bad did the rationing get?" she asked.

"It grew in stages, but it wasn't so bad. Meat, butter and sugar were in short supply over the entire country. I suppose it all depends on how long the war lasts. Technically, the Great War lasted four years, but we really noticed the rationing at the end."

"Four years," Dory said with dismay. Well, maybe it wouldn't be so long this time.

"I spent most of the war at Wallisford Hall, and we didn't really see much of it. In London, though, the Germans came in their great balloons. I never saw them, but we were all terrified one would come, floating to us in complete silence, ready to drop bombs on us."

"It must have been awful."

"The worst was when the letters started coming. Every day there were letters in the village to inform the families of their lost sons. The army took our horses too, as soon as they were ridable. They even took some of our dogs."

"Dogs?"

"I'm not sure why, but they had use of them. My father took to breeding pigeons, too. Everyone had a job, even my father, who bred horses and pigeons. There weren't that many serviceable cars back then—at least not ones that could cover open terrain like horses could, but things are different now."

"I suppose tanks will replace horses."

"I don't know," Lady Pettifer said. "Horses are still extremely versatile. Could be that my brother has been asked to start breeding at Wallisford Hall. If he has, he's probably been asked to keep quiet about it."

Dory listened to everything Lady Pettifer said with both concern and fascination, but they were both distracted by the appearance of a motorcar, and it wasn't Mr. Fernley returning early. It was the same car Dory had seen the night at Lord and Lady Tonbridge, and she knew it belonged to that inspector.

"Who could this be?" Lady Pettifer said, not recognizing the car.

"I believe this might be Inspector Moreau."

They heard Livinia swearing upstairs, and before long, there was a slammed car door and a sharp knock at the door. It was open, along with all windows, to let the air through the building.

"I'll see to him," Dory said as Mr. Fernley wasn't present to perform the duty.

"I suppose you shall have to bring him in here."

Rising, Dory made her way over to the door, where Inspector Moreau stood with his thin frame and straight back. He wore the exact same beige uniform as before, again with his pistol at his side.

"Inspector Moreau," she greeted him.

With a snap, he opened his notebook. "I shall need to speak to yourself," he consulted his notebook, "Miss Sparks, and Miss Fellingworth. Are you both at home?"

"We are. Please come in."

The second policeman he seemed to travel with remained outside as if watching for someone fleeing, ready to give chase at a moment's notice.

Dory led the man into the salon where Lady Pettifer sat. "This is Inspector Moreau," she said, introducing him to the lady. "He is with the gendarmerie. This is Lady Pettifer."

The man gave a sharp bow, but Dory could tell he had no real interest in her. As with DI Ridley, this man only cared about the relevant details of the case.

"Lady Pettifer, you did not attend the soiree at the Lord and Lady Tonbridge house, correct?"

"That is correct," Lady Pettifer said. "Would you like some tea?"

"I will go retrieve Livinia," Dory said and made her way out of the room, to take the wooden staircase up to the second story. Livinia's door was closed and Dory knocked quietly. "That inspector is here. He wishes to speak to you."

The door opened suddenly and Livinia looked sour as if Dory was at fault for bringing her news of their visitor. "I don't know what else I can tell him," she said. "I found him. That's all."

Both returned to the salon, where Inspector Moreau was now sitting uncomfortably in a chair with his legs crossed, the brown leather boots glossy with reflections from the window.

"Miss Fellingworth," he said, rising from his chair. "This is a good time for you tell me everything you know about Baron Drecsay."

Floating down on her seat, Livinia rearranged her skirt, still deeply unimpressed by this interruption. Didn't she realize that her objection to the inconvenience meant nothing to this man. He was hardly going to pack it in because she was annoyed.

"I don't know what else I can tell you," she started.

"When did you meet?"

"Ages ago. I think at a party at Bertie Stringfellow's. We were introduced, but were never really part of the same circle. I've seen him here and there, but we never really knew each other as such," she said with a dismissive wave.

"Yet, you were meeting him in private at the party by Lord and Lady—" He consulted his notes, "Tonbridge."

Livinia's dislike for this interrogation deepened. "He wished to speak in private," was all she said.

"And before that, you were dancing on the dance floor together, no?"

"Yes."

"What was it he wished to say to you in private?"

"How should I know. We never got a chance to speak."

"You must have had some understanding."

"He didn't tell me what was on his mind," Livinia said through gritted teeth.

The inspector looked unimpressed.

"He might have mentioned something about going sailing during the next week," Livinia said, relenting under the inspector's silent pressure. He wrote it down.

"And who was he going sailing with?"

Livinia scratched along her eyebrow for a moment. "That Italian prince… Barenoli, or something some such."

"And you were going with them?"

"No, of course not. I have better things to do than go bob around on some boat."

"Who were his other friends?"

"Like I said, I didn't know him well. Maybe you should talk to Barenoli. He knew him better."

"Have you been to his rooms at Hotel Carlone?"

"No!"

"I think perhaps, Inspector, you are making assumptions where they are not warranted," Lady Pettifer said in a voice with such chill, Dory felt it up her arms. The inspector felt it too. Lady Pettifer stated in no uncertain terms that he was overstepping propriety, and even he, with his investigation, struggled to get past the lady putting her foot down.

Finally, he gave up. "And you, Miss Spark? You knew the man?"

"No, I'm afraid I didn't recognize him in any regard. I'm not sure I've met him before that night."

"He was at the Myrtle party you attended, I believe," Livinia added.

Dory turned her attention back. "If I have met him before, I have no recollection."

"He is a very handsome man."

"Not my kind of handsome," Dory said, refusing to let the blush bloom up her face. But he really wasn't.

Chapter 8

They didn't hear again about the murder for quite a while. Their days returned to normal and Livinia even returned to her social activities—spurred on by Richard coming to pick her up for a tennis match. Livinia left the house in a white sleeveless dress that ended right on the knee, her racquet tucked under her arm.

"I'll be gone for a while. Might be back for dinner, but start without me if I'm not."

The tribulations of the last week had now rolled off her completely and she was swiftly returning to normal. It couldn't be said that she was crushed by Baron Drecsay's death, which showed that she didn't have any deep and lasting feelings for the man.

Maybe what she protested, that she didn't know the man well, was true. Still, Dory felt there was something untoward about the man and his interest in Livinia. It was only his handsome face that would tempt Livinia to stray out of her strict social circle, where status, family and connections mattered. At this point, Dory was learning to see the benefit of it in terms of protecting someone like Livinia from people with less than honorable ambitions.

It was more than Richard's words on the issue now. Lady Pettifer had returned from an afternoon tea with one of the older ladies who lived on the coast with her son, where it had been mentioned that the man did have a reputation for seeking to assure his fortunes. Wealthy heiresses were definitely the kind of women who he kept company with.

With a sigh, Dory tried to dismiss all this from her thoughts. She'd been down this road before and knew how absorbing it could be, gathering and analyzing all information and trying to reach an understanding of what had happened. It wasn't a lie to say that Dory had lost her job, her standing and her friends the last time she had gotten herself caught up in the investigation of a murder. This one she should leave to Inspector Moreau. There was no doubt in her mind that he would absolutely not want her help.

"Why don't you go for a walk, my dear?" Lady Pettifer said. Dory could tell she was tired. "I'll have a little sojourn while you do."

"Alright," Dory said and grabbed her hat. It was early afternoon and the sun was harsh. It didn't have the full heat of August, when it was nearly unbearable with scorching heat built up in the masonry of the house, day after day. The days were still pleasant and Dory walked over the vast lawns to the gardens.

She sought the bench in the garden, where she could sit and stare out at the blue sea. Fishing boats floated in the distance. They weren't so active this time of day, their crew likely sleeping. Dory had never gotten the hang of the siesta, unable to settle down to sleep in the middle of the day. Some days she wished she could sleep away the hottest hours, but her body refused.

So, it was easier to come down here and languish in the garden, or sometimes down by the sea. Below her was a croppy sea shore. It wasn't a bad spot for swimming on the hottest days. A small jetty and a ladder had been built to access the sea, but it wasn't a good place to moor a boat. The rocks were too big and too close, and anything moored there risked being smashed to pieces if the wind picked up.

A lovely breeze came off the sea and she smelled fresh saltiness. The perfume of the flowers around her scented the air as well. In truth, this was a wild garden, left to tend itself most of the time. Dory much preferred it to the neatly trimmed and planned garden at Wallisford Hall, but it was an entirely different thing.

The coast also had citrus. Oranges and lemons that sat like heavy jewels on trees. They were marvelous. Apparently, their lemons were later blooming than most varieties, but they had a more subtle taste. Right now, they weren't ripe.

Dory enjoyed the garden, but she was a little more like Livinia in that she couldn't bring herself to care about the details of gardening and learning the different varieties of plants. Lady Pettifer had a long memory with her garden, remembering the plants and when they were planted, even whom they were planted in honor of.

Dory's mother had only ever invested in one struggling rose bush that against all diversity managed a bloom every other year. It was a tribute to a fallacy of having both the time and inclination to be a gardener, rather than a true passion for her mother, who really was too busy to care for a rose bush as well. Dory smiled at the thought. She did miss home.

For a moment, Dory considered if she should walk to the village, perhaps purchase one of the small bars of chocolate they sold at the village store. It was an indulgence she allowed herself every once in a while. Then she grew worried about the thought of some of these luxury items growing short in supply. Perhaps her love of chocolate would be something she would have to sacrifice to this war.

A renewed discomfort washed over her, like it did every time she thought of the fact that they were at war. Each night, they listened to the BBC and to the relentless German march across Europe. Around here, though, it wasn't the Germans that terrified the population, but the Italians. They were so very close to the border and Mussolini made discomforting noises, and if anyone was to come marching into town, it would be them. The very thought of it was difficult to contemplate. How could life change so quickly? Soldiers coming to disrupt and take control over a region.

What kind of life would they have if the Italians marched into town? They had no great love for the British. There would be a scramble to flee. But so far, no one had come marching across the Italian Alps. Or would they come by sea like the Germans did? Would she wake up one morning and a battalion full of them would be on their doorstep? Dory shuddered.

*

Livinia did return for supper, still dressed in her tennis whites. A grass stain was prominent on one of her knees, and her nose and cheeks were golden with additional sun. She had skin that could take the sun, turning her skin golden. Dory didn't.

"You won't believe what they are saying in town," Livinia said as she sat down at the table, having changed for supper. Her eyes were lit up with excitement. "That Baron Drecsay had a hidden life and that he was killed for spying for the Italians. I don't believe a word of it, but there are those saying it."

"A spy?" Lady Pettifer said. "That's a little far-fetched, isn't it?"

"Considering he's been here for years. What in the world could he be spying on down here? Although, technically, he's part English, they also said. Tied to the Elmhurst family. I had no idea. Like I keep telling everyone, I didn't actually know him. But a spy, can you imagine?"

Both Dory and Lady Pettifer sat in silence for a moment. Yes, the newspapers were full of talk of spies, but for there to actually be one in their midst, at a party they had attended—that seemed preposterous. Could it be? Dory had to question herself. Could it be that he was a spy and was murdered for being found out? "Surely if he was a spy, they would have dragged him away to be questioned somewhere?"

"He was friends with that Prince Barenoli, who is definitely Italian."

"Few amongst the Italian nobility are friends with that upstart Mussolini," Lady Pettifer said. "One cannot jump to the conclusion that being Italian means one is favorable to either Mussolini or the fascists. The world is more complicated than that."

"Well, not everyone seems that way inclined," Livinia said. "And Hungary has displayed a cozy relationship with the Nazis."

Dory could hear someone else's words coming out of Livinia, because never in a thousand years would she care about such politics if there wasn't a murder involved.

"It's never that simple," Lady Pettifer said. "We can't simply label people sympathetic because of where they're from."

"Still, we've locked up every German in the region," Livinia countered.

Lady Pettifer only sighed. "Unless there is some evidence that he was spying, we cannot treat assertions that he was a spy, and murdered for it, as anything more than rumor."

"And really, would it be appropriate to dispatch a spy at Lady Tonbridge's party?" Dory said.

"Perhaps they took their chance as soon as they could out him?"

"Who?" Lady Pettifer demanded.

"The people looking for spies."

"They're hardly going to be at Lady Tonbridge's party, are they?"

"Who's to say? With the Duke and Duchess of Windsor here, who's to say what kind of hidden military men are lurking around the place? They would definitely act if they came across an embedded spy."

Again Dory heard someone else's words coming out of Livinia's mouth. "We can't assume anything. If there is no proof, there is no fact. Assumptions only mean mistakes." Now she heard DI Ridley's sentiments coming out of her own mouth. "Unless there is something actually proving he's a spy, then it's pure speculation. We have to stick to the facts."

"Which are: someone knocked him over the head at a party."

"So we know it was someone at the party," Lady Pettifer stated.

Chapter 9

Dory had to drive whenever Lady Pettifer came in the car, because Lady Pettifer much preferred it to Lavinia's driving, and Dory couldn't blame her. Lavinia's driving was nerve-wracking for anyone. The road along the coast was winding, with tight corners around the dramatic sheer cliffs. They arrived at the Promenade de Anglaise shortly after noon.

It had taken about an hour and a half to get there, and they were set to meet some friends of Lady Pettifer's in a café along the esplanade, and perhaps wander around some of the shops afterward. Lady Pettifer was in need of new stockings.

It wasn't often that they came to Nice, as it was a bit of a drive, but it was nice to venture away from the house every once in a while. Nice was cosmopolitan compared to the small village of St. Tropez. Even though a good portion of residents had gone back to their respective countries, there was no vast absence of people walking along the promenade, and the cafés were patronised enough.

A parking space was available near the Café de Flore, which was situated on a corner. Cane chairs covered the walkway outside of the Café, encircling small white marble tables. It was quite busy with most tables taken. Multiple languages were heard—Dory identified French, Portuguese and English. With Nice being so busy, it was hard to imagine that so much of the population was now absent. On the streets, it didn't seem so, but perhaps it was less busy than a year ago.

"Finally we're here. You really do drive like an old woman, Dory," Lavinia said as she contorted herself out of the back of the car. With sharp strokes, she straightened her skirt. "I hate sitting in the back. My knees always end up in awkward positions and my skirt crumbles up." There was plenty of space in the back; Lavinia was just annoyed that Dory was asked to drive instead of her.

"I better go call Richard," she continued. "I'll only be a moment, so go ahead without me. I'll catch up." She ran off toward the telephone booth further down the street, while Dory helped Lady Pettifer out of the car.

They walked to the café, where Lady Pettifer spotted her party. "There," she said indicating toward the far side, where in a shaded corner, close to the building itself, sat two elderly women, waving when they spotted the new arrivals.

Lady Pettifer made the introductions. A Lady Summernot and Miss Greer. The women shared a resemblance, so Dory assumed they were sisters.

"Is Lavinia not joining us today?" one of the ladies asked, looking disappointed.

"She's here. Simply making arrangements by telephone. You know the young girls," Lady Pettifer said. "They can't simply do one thing in a day, they have to do several. She's planning the rest of her afternoon as we speak."

The women chuckled lightly and indicated to seats for Dory and Lady Pettifer.

"And how are you, Dory?" Miss Greer asked.

"Well. It was a lovely drive."

The waiter, dressed rather informally without a jacket approached, his hair neatly combed and he smiled beneath his trimmed mustache.

"Tea I think," Lady Pettifer said. "Darjeeling, if you have any."

"I'll have the same," Dory added and the other two agreed.

"The temperature is certainly getting warmer. Not quite intolerable yet." Lady Summernot stated. "We do get the sea breezes, so we are not as badly off as some, but I've had to bring some of my more delicate flowers inside."

Miss Greer shifted in her seat. "We were awfully surprised to hear about that unfortunate incident with the Hungarian man. It's so shocking."

"To think something like that would happen here," Lady Summernot added. "This is such a safe place. It's distressing to hear any such news. Poor man. I understand he has no family here. I don't actually know if he has any family at all."

"I did hear that Lavinia found the body," Miss Greer said. "I hope she's not too distressed by it."

"That has made it around, has it?" Lady Pettifer asked. The two ladies were looking at her expectantly, hoping she would enlighten them further. "Lavinia was returning from the powder room when she saw the poor man lying on the floor in the study, bashed about the head."

Technically it was true, but Lavinia *had* been going to the study to meet the man. The powder room was nowhere near the study, and she couldn't simply have been walking past on her way back. Lavinia had definitely been seeking him out, but it wasn't something that Lady Pettifer wanted these women to talk about. Even Dory had heard that these two were notorious gossips, and anything that came out of their mouths, would be known throughout the entire coast.

"It is very curious, though. I knew the man. Very charming. The kind of handsome that you know would lead a man into trouble," Lady Summernot said knowingly.

"He looked just like Rudolph Valentino," Miss Greer said wistfully. "It's all such a shame."

"From what I understand, they haven't found the culprit yet," added Lady Summernot. "But I gather the police have determined it was a cuckolded husband, an enraged and jealous man being responsible for the act. It seems our Baron Drecsay had been caught in a bedroom or two in his time. So he had more than one enemy amongst the husbands around here. It goes to reason that one of them decided to take their fury out on the man himself."

"That's only conjecture, though," Lady Pettifer added.

"Well this was heard said by the regional head for the gendarmerie himself, so there must be some truth to it. At least that is the direction that the police inquiry had led them to."

Lady Pettifer and Dory exchanged looks. This was news to them. They had heard nothing about an irate husband, but then they were quite far away from the gossip and the tattling tongues of Nice and Cannes.

"Is it a police inquiry or a gendarmerie inquiry? Why do the French have to be difficult and have two police forces? It's so confusing," Lady Summernot added.

"We heard it said by some that he is suspected of being a spy," Dory said and both of the women went silent as their attention turned to her.

"Some are seeing spies around every corner, aren't they?" Miss Greer finally said. "If he were a spy, he was certainly a flamboyant one. I would have thought spies were supposed to blend in and go unnoticed, but Baron Drecsay was anything but."

"It's much more likely that he was caught climbing out of some bedroom or other," Lady Summernot said with amusement in her voice. "He was a lively boy, that one."

"Hello, ladies," Lavinia said brightly as she sat down.

"Has your afternoon been planned out then?" queried Lady Summernot.

"Well, I have just found out what everyone else is up to. Myrtle is having a bit of a pool party at her house later this afternoon. So I wonder if you could drop me off on the way home," Lavinia said, turning her attention to Lady Pettifer and Dory.

"Of course," Lady Pettifer said.

It seemed that Lavinia was being embraced back into her crowd, having survived the ordeal of finding a body in the study at Lady Tonbridge's party.

"It's so awfully hot," Lavinia said, fanning herself with the menu from the table.

It was true that it was heating up significantly in the afternoons, but it wasn't properly summer yet. Likely they were heading for a very hot summer. Or perhaps Lavinia's mind was on the refreshing depths of Myrtle's pool.

"It's such a beautiful day," said Miss Greer, looking around as if just noticing the weather. "We are packing, of course."

"Oh, you're returning to England?" Lady Pettifer asked.

"Well, we have a few more weeks," Lady Summernot said, "but with all the trouble we are hearing on the wireless, we thought we'd better head back to England."

"Others were having endless trouble booking passage," Miss Greer added. "The passenger lines aren't running like they used to. We thought we'd head down to the booking office later this afternoon. It can't be as bad as people say."

"The blockades must be stopping some ships from coming through. No doubt the Navy had commandeered some of the passenger traffic."

"Well, people must still travel," Miss Greer said. "Otherwise we understand some are driving all the way to Calais. I'd hate for that to be the only way to return to England."

"There are still ships sailing," Lady Summernot said. "Perhaps we need to look at booking passage from Marseilles instead."

"I wish they would have communicated the difficulty in booking passage more. If we'd known it would be so difficult, we would have left earlier. But there's been nothing. We haven't heard a thing."

"I'm sure they're not willing to broadcast exactly what's happening with the ships in the area," Lady Pettifer said quietly.

"You don't think the ships are at risk, do you? Nothing's happened so far." Grave concern registered in Miss Greer's face.

"At wartime, there's always a risk."

"Surely they wouldn't interfere with civilian ships?"

"I hope not," Lady Summernot said. "Passenger transport was quite safe during the last war. I doubt even the Germans would sink so low as to torpedo a civilian ship. I think interfering even with merchant ships is a crime. Doing so with the passenger ships, civilian ships, would be an atrocity. Not even the Germans could be that unreasonable."

By the look of Lady Pettifer's expression, Dory knew that she wasn't convinced. Lady Pettifer rarely gave the Germans the same benefit of the doubt as others did. Even her brother, Lord Wallisford, was a little bit more blasé about the Germans, while the Lady Pettifer was deeply concerned about this war, and her suspicions about their safety ran to everything. Dory could only hope she was wrong. It was distressing to think that civilian ships would be targeted as part of the military operations, but they couldn't deny it was a risk.

"I hate all this talk about the war and the Germans," Lavinia stated. "They're not breaching the French lines and that's that. I wish we could all stop talking about it."

Lady Pettifer gave her a circumspect look, almost pitying. Although Dory wished dearly that Lavinia was right. The Germans were moving north because they could, but they wouldn't come this far south as Italy and the French were holding them to the east. Hopefully the Germans had been hemmed in enough to have done all the damage they could at this point.

Chapter 10

The house of Lavinia's friend sat at the top of a very steep hill and a small cable car led from the garage down by the coast road, reaching up through the trees covering the side of the hill. Dory pulled over and Lavinia got out, telling them not to wait up. In a way, Lavinia almost looked relieved escaping their company. She didn't always hide how bored she was with them.

In the slowly rising cable car, she looked a small and lonely figure, inching her way up the side of the hill.

With a wave, Dory pulled away and they continued driving down the road toward St. Tropez.

"What do you think of what Lady Summernot said about the police having concluded some wronged husband had killed Baron Drecsay?" Dory asked.

Lady Pettifer sat quietly for a moment as if considering the idea. "It's hard to say as there's no particular husband anyone can point to. I'm sure the man was no saint, but if passions were so inflamed that they led to murder, wouldn't we know more about it?"

"The theory does sound possible, but you're right, there seems to be no evidence to back it up. At least not anything we've come across. Do you think the police could know something and are refusing to tell anyone?"

"I doubt it. Can't hide anything in a place like this," Lady Pettifer said. "If there was something going on, it would certainly not be quiet. And if he were in the thick with some lover, would he really be sniffing around Lavinia the way he was?"

"Maybe that was a distraction from an affair he was having, a means to deflect attention?"

"If a man were to murder his wife's lover, it's more likely because the news was emerging about it."

"Or perhaps there was blackmail involved," Dory said.

"This is all pure speculation. Speculation means nothing without proof."

"It must be that the police have no proof, otherwise they would've arrested someone by now if there was any truth to their suspicions. Provided their suspicions are correct to begin with."

"I'm sure if Lady Summernot is talking about it, there could well be some truth to it. She is very good at garnering what is true and what is not. I'll give her that. The woman has a good fifty years' experience with receiving and conveying tidbits about the people around here," Lady Pettifer said dryly.

Biting her lip, Dory had to wonder if there were some unpleasant turns in the history between Lady Pettifer and Lady Summernot. On first appearance, they seemed very friendly, but when studying closer, Dory could see that there was tension between the ladies, at least from Lady Pettifer's side. It wasn't her place to dwell about things like that. If Lady Pettifer wanted to inform her of any past transgressions, she would.

Picking a piece of lint off her skirt, Lady Pettifer sighed. "My worry, though, is that the French Police will not look into it further. Like Miss Greer said, 'people are seeing spies in every shadow,' and that is probably true for the police as well. They would be much more concerned about the potential of military presence in the area."

"It is a murder," Dory said emphatically.

"Yes, but it sounds as though the police have no real clue as to who the culprit is. Their assertion that it was a wronged husband must come from assumptions they've made based on Baron Drecsay's character—potentially without any real proof. It's been almost two weeks now, and they haven't apprehended anyone. That worries me."

In silence, Dory considered what this meant. The police were taking their time finding the person responsible. For a moment, she had to wonder if DI Ridley would be more vigilant in his investigation than the French Police appeared to be. The French always had a standoffish attitude to the foreigners here on the coast. They often left any issues for the consulates to take care of.

Technically, the consulates weren't mandated, or even equipped, to investigate murders, and it certainly wasn't within their jurisdiction. It seemed the French Police had done their bit and concluded they could not find the culprit.

Perhaps that was a little ungenerous. The inspector was surely following up on any leads he had. But from what Lady Summernot was saying, no particular lover of this baron had come forth. Either they were very discreet or this man wasn't quite the Lothario that people were making him out to be.

There was no doubt he was a handsome man, and people had naturally assumed he had a lascivious character because of it. It might not be true. He might not be crawling around every bedroom on the coast, even if he had the looks to do so. It was imprudent to assume this was part of his character simply by the way he looked.

One never assumed that beauty was something that would be problematic for people, but apparently their looks got in the way as people made assumptions based on them. Beauty was always assumed to be a wondrous asset, but perhaps it could be a detriment at times too. People always assume certain characteristics went along with that beauty—spoilt, vapid and entitled.

With these thoughts, Dory felt ashamed because she had also assumed attributes based on nothing other than how he looked. She was as guilty as others of expecting that a pretty face translated to a simple and easy life. This man, Drecsay, deserved the same level of justice as anyone else who found themselves a victim of an egregious crime. The man had lost his life. No one deserved that, and no one deserved such a crime to go unpunished.

"I do recall someone saying he was quite close to a Countess Tirau," Dory said. "Did you know her?"

"Everyone knew her," Lady Pettifer replied. "She is not the brightest woman, one has to admit. Petty at times. She would likely be swayed by someone like Drecsay if he was charming to her."

"I can't quite recall who said it, I think it was Richard, but he said that Countess Tirau treated him indulgently, almost like a son."

The car was silent for a moment and Lady Pettifer seemed to consider the thought, worrying her lip between her fingers. "I shouldn't think they were lovers. She was an elderly woman. It certainly would be unseemly if it were true. We don't know if he profited at all from her death."

"It would be good to find out," Dory agreed. "Although if he had profited greatly and Countess Tirau's family were aggrieved by it, that could be motive for murder. Still, I would have assumed there'd have been quite a scandal if that were the case."

"A bequeathment like that would've been taken to court, and I can't see a court being favorable to some Lothario charming inheritances out of an elderly lady. I haven't heard of any gossip to that effect. Lady Summernot would absolutely have mentioned it. Still, it is the strongest connection that has been mentioned with regards to this man. The problem is that we don't know him that well. He could have been getting up to anything—but the gossip mongers were apparently not hearing about it."

"Some people are very discreet," Dory stated.

"A man like that, though, is noticed wherever he goes. There is a curious lack of gossip about anything substantial related to this murder. All speculation and no facts."

"You don't think he could be a homosexual?" Dory asked. That community was notoriously discreet about their activities, collectively watching out for each other as they bore risks simply by associating.

"He would clearly have been a part of a certain crowd if that were true. I suppose it could be," Lady

Pettifer said after a while. For a while longer she was silent. "It would be a shame if the police stopped investigating at this point. The man does deserve his justice."

*

They arrived home just before dusk, walking into a mercifully still and silent house after the busy day. Lady Pettifer was tired by the day's activities, even if they'd only sat in the car or at a café for most of it. In the end, they had forgone finding stockings, and had instead returned home. It was still a draining day that Lady Pettifer sat down heavily in her favorite chair as soon as she reached it.

Supper wouldn't be far away and they simply sat and enjoyed the silence for a while before shifting to the dining room. There was no doubt that Lady Pettifer would retire early that night to recuperate from the day. As for Dory, there was still an unpleasant heaviness to her thoughts regarding this man and his death.

It felt as if justice was improperly being done. Just because there was a war didn't mean he should be forgotten and swept under the carpet because his death was inconvenient. Or because he was a foreigner in this land. Surely the police hadn't given up. Still, Dory couldn't escape the heavy feeling that had descended on her, because she suspected that his murder was deemed too inconvenient to deal with at this time, and that went against the grain.

Chapter 11

Livinia sighed as she stood by the window in the salon. Apparently, the news that some cuckolded husband was responsible for Baron Drecsay's murder had spread across the entire coast, and it seemed to have been accepted as truth, even without a scrap of evidence.

"It's as if everyone is ready to sweep the whole incident under the carpet," Livinia said. "Either some husband, or they are saying the authorities are essentially ignoring the case because he really was a spy."

"Some people will believe anything," Lady Pettifer said.

Grabbing one of the small cucumber sandwiches, Dory sat back in the chair and took a bite, chewing it carefully while she thought. "To be fair, quite a few of the aristocracy admire the fascists."

"Posh," Lady Pettifer said.

"Come on, Aunt. There are even quite a few who think Hitler is simply marvelous."

"I wouldn't go that far."

Dory frowned, wondering if Lady Pettifer was applying her own views on others. Dory had heard those sympathizers speaking at Wallisford Hall. They couldn't all have changed their minds because Britain had declared war. "In Italy, families have profited from aligning themselves with Mussolini. It must be that many in Hungary are hedging their bets by making themselves agreeable to the

Nazis. I suppose it would be understandable. If Hungary manages to convince the Nazis that they are aligned with their principles, maybe they will spare themselves being invaded by them."

"If he were a spy, he would hardly be spending time at parties dancing with me, would he?" Livinia stated. "Besides, people with Nazi sympathies seem incapable of keeping quiet about it."

"He would if he were a spy," Dory said.

If he were, it's hard to see what he would gain by aligning himself with Livinia. It's not as though anyone of particular importance to the war effort is part of her inner circle. Granted, many have important and influential relatives, but being on the other side of Europe, it's hard to see how that could be of any use.

"There's no point sitting here speculating," Lady Pettifer said. "What does this Prince Barenoli say?"

Silence settled on the room.

"I'm sure the police spoke to him," Livinia said after a while.

"And the friends of Countess Tirau," Lady Pettifer continued. "I did not know her well. I'm not even sure where she was from. She wasn't amongst my friends, but she would have had some. I'm sure Baron Drecsay wasn't the only acquaintance she had."

"I suppose we could ask," Livinia said and they all looked from one to another.

"It's not really our place to ask," Dory said.

Lady Pettifer chuckled. "Could you really rein in your curiosity enough not to investigate?"

Biting her lip, Dory silently fumed that her curiosity was so very obvious. It was true. She would find it impossible not to pay attention if someone mentioned anything related to Drecsay.

"Besides, the police seem to have utterly lost interest in the poor man's death," Lady Pettifer continued. "If he is related to the Elmhursts, then I know his grand aunt. It wouldn't feel right not at least trying to urge the authorities to solve this murder."

"Perhaps we could speak to this prince," Livinia said. "I might as well find out where he lives."

*

For the second time in the week, they drove along the winding road to Nice. Lady Pettifer stayed home, her knee giving her trouble. This time, Livinia insisted on driving and Dory clutched the side of the door during the sharpest turns.

"Most of the princes I've met have been old," Livinia said, "but if he's a friend of Drecsay, he must be quite young."

"I suppose so."

"Drecsay never mentioned him much. I really didn't know Drecsay well," Livinia said earnestly, looking over to gauge Dory's expression. "But heavens was he handsome. Those dark eyes. Sent a shiver down my spine. I can't believe someone killed him. It's such a shame."

As they arrived, Livinia pulled in by one of the large Victorian structures along the Promenade de Anglais with massive white columns and impossibly large windows along the front. It was the Palais de la Méditerranée and a velvet liveried man came forward to open the car door for them. He bid them welcome with a smile and prepared to drive the car away somewhere more convenient.

A darkly dressed man approached them as they entered the lovely lobby of the hotel, decorated with arts décoratifs motifs. Everything in the hotel was modern and of the highest taste. This prince had money. Of that, there was no question. Yet he was friends with a man who was basically considered to be in gentile poverty. Wealth didn't always count for everything, and it stood in this prince's favor that he would be friends with a man of much fewer means—unless it was a relationship built on a common mission to uncover information for their governments.

Dory was increasingly curious about this baron and how he was with his friends and the world around him. How did one identify a spy?

They were directed to an elevator built of rich cherry wood and brass. An operator dressed in red asked who they sought and then proceeded to get the elevator moving.

The carpet in the corridor was cream with flowers and the walls had silk coverings with tropical leaves. Every part of this hotel was stunning.

They arrived at a large, white door and knocked.

"Miss Fellingworth," a man said as he opened the door. "I have been expecting you." Like his friend, this man was dark and beautiful, and he moved with the grace of a man who knew his place in the world. There was an assurance, almost a boredom as he led them in into a sumptuous room, walking past a man who proceeded to close the door behind them. Dory guessed he was a manservant.

The prince sat down on a white brocade sofa and crossed his legs. His waistcoat was unbuttoned and he looked a little less than ready to receive visitors, even if he clearly knew they were coming.

"I know who you are, of course," he said, his attention on Livinia. "You are the one who found Domenik." The man had dark eyebrows that flared elegantly across his face. Dark hair neatly combed in a side part, displaying a uniform wave to his hair.

"Yes. I knew him a little."

The prince rubbed his thumb across his lower lip as he considered her and from her seat, Dory could almost feel Livinia's cheeks burning with the attention. The baron and his friend, the prince, had good looks in common. As for Dory, she was wondering if this man in front of her could in any way have been induced to kill his friend.

"We were hoping you could tell us a little about him," Dory stated after a while. "There are so many rumors about him. The police seem to have made some assumptions about his death."

"The police," the prince said with a hint of disgust in his voice, "couldn't find a whore in a whorehouse."

Okay, Dory said to herself. "There are some who suspect he was a spy." On second thought, was that a stupid question to ask? A spy wouldn't confirm it, would they? "Or that he was murdered by some irate husband. As you are his friend, would you know of any such husband that was particularly upset?"

"Husbands of beautiful wives are always upset. That is the cost of beauty."

The man spoke in generalizations. Well, that was helpful. "Any specific ones that you know of?"

The man shrugged. "Not that he told me."

"And Countess Tirau?" Livinia said.

"They were friends. She enjoyed beauty. There was a price." With a sigh, he shifted slightly as if to alleviate his boredom. "Drecsay was a proud man. He was not a man to accept charity. Still, he found the bills a little harder to pay once the countess passed away."

"So there was no one new to take the countess' place?"

"You mean in his affections?"

Dory got the distinct impression that this man was toying with her, and she didn't understand what it meant. Men like him, men with power and wealth did have a tendency to toy with people. She'd seen it before. Vivian Fellingworth was a little like that. They tended to use the truth as a blunt instrument to beat people with. Was he merciless with Drecsay because of his... solution to his problems?

"The countess was an indulgent woman, but only when it pleased her. She liked to yank the chain at times, ensure he knew who held the reins. Some people use wealth as a means to control. If he displeased her, his debts would build up and she would threaten not to pay them." He certainly wasn't sugar-coating his friend's position. "So was he discreetly visiting the bedrooms of some of the more beautiful members of society here? Absolutely. But he was discreet. Couldn't have the countess finding out.

"Financial difficulties aside, the countess' death released some chains. The countess didn't like him showing interest in the younger ladies of the coast." His attention was back on Livinia as if accenting his point. This man knew of Drecsay's interest in Livinia, Dory bet.

"Financially, though, the death of his benefactor would have been devastating," Dory said and slowly, the Prince stole his attention away and settled on her.

He blatantly studied her for a moment. "He wasn't overly distressed. I don't know the details, but he was very positive about his future, stated that he had secured a way to rebuild his family wealth."

This surprised Dory. Surely, he hadn't meant Livinia, but she was an heiress. "Did he elaborate, or was this something he stated quite often?"

"Are you asking if he was some dreamer who constantly thought up schemes to re-establish the family wealth? Or are you asking if he saw young Miss Fellingworth here as the means to securing his future?"

His assertion was too forward for her to answer, and he knew it.

"Nothing about me was secured," Livinia added loftily. "We barely knew each other. I don't know why I have to keep telling people."

The prince returned his gaze to Dory as if this should provide her with an answer. But it didn't. "Was he a dreamer?" Dory pressed.

"No, he was not. I would go so far as to say some of his actions were the result of desperation, but he wasn't a stupid man—a dreamer. He was very... calculated in his actions. And he did enjoy dealing with Countess Tirau. She might have used her wealth with bluntness, but he had finesse. It was a mutually beneficial arrangement."

"No threats?"

"Have you set yourself the task of investigating his murder?"

"Yes," Dory said frankly and a hint of emotion quickly fleeted across the prince's face.

"And what authority do you have to do so?"

"None. We simply feel the police are not giving this case their due attention."

"There are also some duties felt to his family," Livinia added. The prince only glanced at her. He seemed to have lost interest in her to focus more on studying Dory.

The man's eyebrows rose. "I understand part of his background is English. The English do like to stick together, as you say. Is that why you are here? You feel a duty to him because of his family?" He was speaking directly to Dory.

"No," she said.

"Then why?"

"Because no one deserves to have their life stolen."

"So melodramatic." His eyes traveled down her clothes and shoes. "Your accent is English, but not educated."

Dory blushed as he kept studying her. "Yet here you are. What brings you so far away from your country?"

"I am a companion to Lady Pettifer."

"My aunt."

"Ah," the prince said as if everything made sense now. "And here you are, investigating the murder of some foreigner who wouldn't give you the time of day had you asked." With a frown, Dory tried to understand what this man was saying. He spoke in riddles, eluding to things without actually saying them. "You are an idealist."

Dory had never really put labels on what she was, but perhaps she was. "Someone must be, I suppose."

The prince regarded her some more and then looked away. "I must prepare now. It has been charming to meet you both, but my time is valuable."

"Of course," Livinia said and rose. Dory was less impressed. Could he spare so little time to the people trying to find justice for his murdered friend? Or had he lost interest because he didn't believe they would achieve anything. The comment about Drecsay not giving the time of day to someone like her stuck. Having mentioned it, Prince Barenoli obviously wasn't unaware of the sentiment. Perhaps he felt the same way.

Chapter 12

The drive back was done in silence. Dory was trying to sort through all of the prince's assertions, accusations and euphemisms. At times, Dory wasn't entirely sure he had been trying to be straight with them, having both disparaged and maligned his friend. But they had learned more about the relationship between the baron and the countess that was his patroness. The assertion that she paid his bills was clear, and he had struggled financially after her death. Also, the baron believed he had some means of restoring his wealth. This did not signify that he had inherited anything substantial from the countess.

"What a curious man," Livinia said. "Very handsome."

Dory rolled her eyes. The man had an acerbic personality. Intelligent but supercilious. There was even something a bit jaded about him. For his honeyed smile, he was in character much too dark for someone like Livinia.

"He wasn't married. Did you see? No ring on his finger."

"That doesn't mean he's not married," Dory said with weariness. Livinia had a habit of being persuaded by the superficial. This man's surface sold a prince charming, but the personality underneath was anything but. The fact that he had counted Baron Drecsay as a friend, despite the difference in their means, pointed to there being some commonality to their characters that gave them common ground.

Were they spies, though? There was too much arrogance there to bow to fascists. Or maybe he was enough of a realist to align himself to the direction the wind was blowing. It would be a mistake to think she knew what it would take to turn someone into a spy.

*

A car was parked in front of the house as they arrived home. Dory had never seen it before. Pulling next to it, Livinia got out. "Who can that be?"

An uncomfortable feeling crept up Dory's spine and at that moment, she heard Vivian's voice drifting out of the open window. Dory sighed. Lady Pettifer laughed at something he said. As dreadful as he was, Lady Pettifer adored him. Dreadful wasn't the exact word; how Dory felt about him was more complex. He could be very charming, but that was simply a mask. Underneath, he actually was quite dreadful—but also observant and insightful when not obtusely disregarding.

The last time she'd seen him, he'd called her a meddling oik and the insult still stung. Biting her lips together, she automatically checked her hair before following Livinia inside the house.

"Vivian!" Livinia said, gleeful in seeing him when Dory knew they had a contentious relationship—but then siblings always did, and these two were twins, which had to constitute some bond she didn't understand. They certainly weren't best friends.

"Hello, chook," he said and Livinia gave him a pointed look. They embraced, which might be the only time Dory had seen that, but then they had been apart for two years. "And Miss Sparks," he said with a quirky tone to his voice. He kissed her on the cheek, leaving a lingering whiff of maleness and whiskey.

Kissing her on the cheek as greeting was something new too. There had been a time when he'd appeared quite eager to explore her form in some hidden closet, but kissing her on the cheek for greeting wasn't something he did. Perhaps it had something to do with her elevated status as a companion rather than a mere maid.

Even so, there had never been a time when Vivian hadn't made her feel uncomfortable, and he'd done so purposefully on more than one occasion.

"Vivian was telling me about his drive from Switzerland," Lady Pettifer.

"How is Mother?" Livinia asked as she sat down.

For a moment, Dory didn't know what to do with herself, if she should leave them to their familial discussion.

"She's fine," he said.

Apparently that was enough for Livinia, who Dory knew had quite mixed feelings about her mother. She wasn't as readily forgiving as Vivian seemed to be. "You'll never guess what happened here," she said with wide, excited eyes. "There was a murder and I found the body."

Gingerly, she sidestepped the issue that she had been meeting this man for a private assignation. It was a fact that Livinia seemed to have wiped from her memory.

"A murder?" Vivian stated with surprise. "You must be right in your element," he said to Dory, who couldn't find anything to respond with and simply sat there opening and closing her mouth.

"We are investigating," Livinia continued. "Today we questioned his best friend, a Prince Barenoli. An utterly fascinating man. So charming and handsome—you wouldn't believe it. He really is keeping up the standard of the fairy tales."

"Did you find him charming?" Vivian asked, turning his attention to Dory. With that, everyone turned their attention to her, effectively forcing her to answer.

"No."

Vivian's eyebrows rose, but he wasn't surprised, and instead had a reassured expression as if he knew her so well. "Won't be swayed by any Prince Charming, will you? Pray tell, why didn't you find the handsome prince charming?"

"Must be the arrogance," she said through gritted teeth. In a way, it sounded petty because he knew that was what she accused him of. "There was something dark about him, something jaded."

"Tosh," Livinia said. "He was lovely, and so happy we were investigating his friend's death."

Vivian didn't take his gaze away from Dory, and she suddenly found the tea service inordinately fascinating, deciding to pour herself a cup of the cooling tea. It had been a long ride and she was parched.

"How was it traveling across the border?" Lady Pettifer asked.

"It was a mess. It took two hours to get them to let me through. Soldiers everywhere. It seems the French are worried the Swiss are going to roll over for Herr Hitler. I saw garrisons camped a bit further inland, endless fields of them. Tanks and rows and rows of sandbags. The French have made themselves ready."

A silence descended on the room.

"And what did you learn about poor Baron Drecsay?" Lady Pettifer said, breaking the uncomfortable silence, as if she'd heard all she could tolerate about the war.

"Well," Livinia said. "He'd been in some financial strife since the death of his benefactor, Countess Tirau, but he believed he'd found some means out of it."

A frown marred Lady Pettifer's face, but Vivian didn't look concerned. But then, he didn't know about this man's interest in Livinia.

"The prince said he was intelligent and that he considered the commitments he made." Livinia was making it all sound too peachy.

"He confirmed that Drecsay had been a visitor to a few bedrooms he shouldn't be in, and that his benefactor frowned deeply if she even found out about it," Dory added, more for Lady Pettifer's benefit.

"Oh, that kind of benefactor," Vivian said as if he now understood. "A kept man."

"Vivian!" Livinia chided. "No need to be crude. The police say that some irate husband dispatched him. Although other people say he was a spy."

"A spy?" Vivian said with amused expression.

"Well, he was Hungarian and their position can only be described as detached."

"What could a spy possibly garner by creeping around bedrooms in Cote d'Azur?" Vivian asked.

"You'd be surprised what people around here know," Lady Pettifer said. "Who here doesn't have a family member in Parliament? I'm sure quite a few even have relatives in the actual War Cabinet."

"That they wish to speak about to a foreign bedroom hustler?"

"He was not a hustler," Livinia stated with offense. "Why do you insist on painting everything in the ugliest light possible?"

"What other light can one put it in? A man patroned by older women. There is only so much light one can use."

"Children," Lady Pettifer said with exasperation. "Now we are very glad you have come to see us. Are you staying a while?"

"I haven't made any specific plans," Vivian said. "Obviously, I need to get back to England, but I hear the passenger ships are getting harder to book passage on."

"Unfortunately, that is true. Speaking to Mrs. Muiring on the phone today, she mentioned that her neighbors were driving to Spain to book passage."

"That would take days," Livinia uttered.

"Don't worry, Vivian," Lady Pettifer said. "We'll find a way home for you, but there is no reason you can't stay a few weeks."

"No, of course not. It's always lovely down here. Spring seems to be late back home, and things are pretty grim there. This malaise seems to have descended everywhere. It's like we're in a war that refuses to be and no one seems to know what's going on. London has turned into a maze of sandbags. I've never seen it so drab."

"Things are gayer here," Livinia said. "Except for this murder. It's shocking. Who could do such a thing? It's as if people are losing their minds everywhere."

"Things are only going to get worse," Vivian said. "And Mother is basically a stone's throw away from Germany. Half of the people who work at the sanatorium are of German descent."

"I doubt the Germans have raiding the sanatoriums of Switzerland utmost on their agenda," Lady Pettifer said. "Still, it is a worry. If the Germans were to invade, the suffering would be indiscriminate."

"They wouldn't take mother hostage, would they?" Livinia said, concern finally registering on her face.

"For what purpose?" Vivian asked.

"I don't know. She is a lady. Maybe they assume she could serve as some leverage."

"What does your father say?" Lady Pettifer asked.

"He refuses to speak about it."

With a snort, Lady Pettifer looked away.

"We must do something about Mother. I just don't know what."

"She's not allowed to leave," Livinia pointed out.

"Yes, thanks, Livinia. I'm fairly sure the sanitorium regulations didn't consider the large-scale invasion by the Germans."

"The French line is holding," Livinia countered. "They will arrest her if she returns to England. That was the deal father struck with the commissioner."

With piercing eyes, Vivian glared at her. Dory couldn't exactly tell what he was thinking.

"Perhaps she needs to be transferred somewhere less volatile," Dory added after a moment of silence.

"There's nowhere that isn't volatile," Vivian said, turning his eyes on her as if she were responsible."

"America," Dory added quietly. "They have absolutely insisted on being neutral in this war, and they are much too far away for the Germans.

"They say Belgium is a bit of a canary in the mine, that the Germans would invade them first, get the small problem tackled before the big problem," Lady Pettifer added. "They might bypass Switzerland entirely. They cannot fight on every border, and Switzerland has never indicated it will serve as a problem for them."

"Would you bet your life on it?" Vivian asked. "Everyone is expecting the invasion to start any day."

A silence descended again, as if no one wanted to say anything more, in case their words brought around the eventuality they all feared.

Chapter 13

Vivian spent a bit of time in his guest room the next day. He slept, Dory assumed. For all his blasé attitude, Dory could tell he was worried, and that worried her. When people like Vivian were taking things seriously, it spelled the situation had to be dire.

Could it be that they had stayed on in France too long? There were still so many here; it was hard to believe they were in grave danger. The heavy militarization Vivian mentioned up north wasn't visible here. Other than the lack of sugar and the half-hearted insistence on blackouts, there was nothing really visible of the war here on the coast.

Most said they were simply going to wait this war out, refusing to be chased out of their house and home to return to cities or families they no longer felt welcome with. Lady Pettifer felt she couldn't endure the travel, and Livinia still feared the remnants of her mother's scandal. But now Dory was frightened.

On the wireless, they reported a great deal of bluster. Communications with the French and agreements to stay strong. Nothing particular was being reported, which on the one hand was excellent, but it almost felt as though the Germans were too quiet, as if they were planning to pounce. Hopefully, Dory was completely overreacting.

Walking outside, she let the gentle morning sun warm her skin. This was the lovely part of the day, before the heat really set in. The breeze coming off the sea was pleasant and there was a stillness. Except for the birds that were chirping away. This place was so lovely. How could something so horrid as war be threatening all around them?

The noise of a car echoed across the trees. Someone had arrived and Dory walked around the corner of the house to see. It was Richard, who was stepping out of his car.

"Has she come down yet?" he asked.

"Livinia? No, I'm afraid not."

He growled slightly. "She told me to come early. I should have known better than to listen to her. But you're up. Trusty Dory. Early to bed, early to rise."

This made Dory wonder what kind of opinion Richard had of her. It wasn't as if she was old enough yet to be considered the dour spinster—not that it strictly mattered what he thought. "Not always, but when I've had a trying day, then yes." And also because Vivian and Livinia had stayed up, and Dory had learned to fear Vivian's tongue when he drank. That was when he tended to be his most vicious and Dory had fled to bed rather than stayed with them. Not that she was going to tell Richard any of this.

"I heard you and Livvie were in Nice yesterday."

"Yes, we met with Prince Barenoli."

"That wanker. Excuse my French."

"I take it he's not your favorite person," Dory said.

"Thinks a lot of himself. Can be a right bastard to the girls. They swoon over themselves for a royal title. It's pathetic."

Dory decided not to mention that Livinia had been in danger of swooning a bit herself. It felt disloyal pointing something like that out, but Richard only confirmed her own impression of the handsome prince. 'Beauty came with a price,' he had said more than once. Maybe he was one to test how much people were willing to pay. He hadn't overtly said anything despicable; it was just a feeling Dory had gotten. With a shake of her head, Dory dismissed the man from her thoughts.

Speaking of low opinions. "You seem to have a very low opinion of Baron Drecsay."

"Really the kind we can do without," Richard said with a disgusted look on his face.

"You mean gentile poor?" Dory said without thinking, or rather without care.

"If you can't afford to be here, you shouldn't be. Sniffing around rich old women. It's disgraceful."

"He was also sniffing around Livinia," Dory pointed out and Richard's mouth tightened. Obviously, Richard was in love with Livinia, but she never quite saw him as anything other than a friend she depended on for just about everything. The truth was that he would probably make her quite a good husband, but she was off being impressed by the superficial beauty of foreign nobles. "Anyone else he was sniffing around?"

"Who knows," Richard stated. "He liked anyone with money. I didn't really know him that well—stayed clear of his lot. Someone who did know him better was Terry Wilcott. They were chums, I suppose. He might be the one who knows who Drecsay was dabbling with. But, you know, I wouldn't dismiss the theory that he was a spy. The man would do anything for money."

"Except spies tend to be carted away and interrogated, not whacked on the head and left at society parties."

Richard's eyebrows rose and sank. "I suppose. Perhaps it is more likely that someone was trying to keep some woman out of the man's clutches."

Which actually gave Richard a motive more than anyone, but by the look on his face, the thought that he was a suspect never occurred to him. At the party, he had claimed to arrive late, but who was to say that was true. It was blatantly clear that Richard had a distaste for the man. He wouldn't be the first person to protect one of the Fellingworth offspring, Dory thought with a snort. It appeared Richard took that snort as agreement with what he was saying.

"Actually, Terry is going to be there this afternoon, maybe you should come along if you want to ask him. Whose is the car?"

"Didn't I tell you? Vivian arrived yesterday."

This time, Richard's eyebrows rose even higher in surprise. "Vivian? It's been an age since I've seen him. Livvie didn't say."

"We weren't expecting him."

"Just like Vivian to go where the wind takes him," Richard said with a smile. "It's been a few years since I've seen him. I don't suppose he is up either?"

"No," Dory said.

"Why is it so hard to get these Fellingworths out of bed?" he said brightly and walked back to the house. "The day is young and the party awaits. Terry is likely to be there. Are you going to come?"

Indecision accosted Dory. The urge to talk to this Terry itched inside her, and she didn't entirely understand why. No one seemed to like this Baron Drecsay, except perhaps Livinia. Even his friends appeared very blasé about his murder. The police seemed to have stopped caring entirely, feeling they had better things to do than investigate the death of some bedroom-creeping foreigner. Maybe it was the fact that no one seemed to care that really got on Dory's wick. You couldn't just wipe someone away and get away with it.

"Lady P," Dory heard from inside the house. "Smashing day."

"Young Richard," Lady Pettifer replied. "Have you come to steal Livinia away for the day. That would be good. She's been a bit blue about that man's unfortunate demise."

Taking a breath, Dory exhaled. Truth be told, she wasn't sure how deeply Livinia cared about Baron Drecsay's murder. At times it felt like only she cared, and she hadn't even met the man.

Fine, she would go speak to this Terry Wilcott, she decided, taking a few more minutes outside. Lady Pettifer didn't need assistance dealing with the charms of men like Richard.

"Well, I'll be damned," Vivian's voice was heard. It was a little gruff with sleep. "Look who the cat dragged in."

"Vivian," Richard said brightly. "How are you?"

Richard seemed to be just as keen on Vivian as he was with his sister. "Good. About to head off to a party at Archie Wilshire's villa."

"Archie? I didn't know he was here. Haven't seen him since Oxford, second year. I thought he went to work for the Colonial Office. I know they call this a colony, but that's a bit of a stretch."

"Things didn't work out so well there, it seems. Too soft to put his foot down."

"That wouldn't surprise me," Vivian replied.

Standing there, Dory felt like she was eavesdropping, but it hadn't been her intention to. With her head up, she made her way to the salon where everyone had gathered.

Vivian looked no worse for wear from the evening before, but little seemed to dampen his overall golden glow.

"I wish Livinia could be a little more like you at times, Dory," Richard stated. "You never linger in bed all day."

"That's because she's used to getting up at the crack of dawn," Vivian said dismissively and walked over to the tea service.

Dory smiled tightly. Oh, it was going to be a lovely day—a full day of bearing the brunt of Vivian's jibes.

"Be nice, Vivian," Lady Pettifer chided.

"I'm always nice, aren't I, Miss Sparks?"

Dory didn't bother answering and Vivian grinned.

Chapter 14

Archie Wilshire had a lovely house built in art décoratif style, entirely white with large, sweeping rooms and enormous windows. It might be the most modern house Dory had ever seen. The furniture was exquisite as well, dainty with beautifully inlaid wood paneling. Dory spent her first moments in the house simply looking at everything. It was a world away from the two up, two down joined house she grew up in, and even miles away from the staid, old elegance of Wallisford Hall. This was a house of jazz and ideas—a complete rejection of all traditions. Dory loved it.

Vivian was immediately greeted by all and sundry. Everyone seemed to know him, but mostly from England rather than any time spent here on the coast. It seemed all the people of his class knew each other—or at least knew Vivian.

A few of the gathered party was dressed in tennis whites, so Dory guessed that part of the afternoon would involve tennis. A large, covered veranda overlooked a pool and the gardens beyond. With a smile, Dory could imagine how much Lady Pettifer would disapprove of this house, with its showy glossiness and blatant self-assurance.

Livinia was alive in this setting, adored by the people and loving being part of her group. She was practically bouncing on her feet as she walked.

"Archie," she said, greeting their host, whom Dory understood was married to an elegant woman who wore silk blouses with long strands of fat pearls. Meredith was her name and she had polished black hair and a small mouth, accentuated by red lipstick.

In this crowd, Dory couldn't help feeling frumpy. As much as she didn't care about being accepted, and the center of attention as Livinia did, she also couldn't muster the self-confidence that this group seemed to thrive on.

"And you remember Dory, of course," Livinia said to the gentleman wearing a cream linen suit. It cut a lovely line on him, but it wrinkled. Still, comfort in this heat was important. "We wanted her to come along. I hope you don't mind."

With gritted teeth, Dory smiled. When she'd agreed to come, she hadn't realized her presence would be hoisted on the host as a favor.

"No, of course not," he said gregariously. No sign of imposition could be seen on his face and Dory liked Archie more for it. "Do you play tennis, Dory?"

"Two left feet," she said. "I will spare everyone the pain of having to watch me chase a ball."

"You and me both," Meredith agreed, taking a sip of an iced drink from a long, slim glass.

With that, the attention was off Dory and they moved onto discuss what they had done over the last few years. Archie was an ardent sailor, and apparently Meredith could watch him out at sea from the cool of the veranda.

If Archie wasn't so very foreign to Dory, she dared to think she would muster a crush on him. He was kind and generous, and smiled a great deal—but he was also so different from her, she wasn't entirely sure she read him right. Could he really be that nice? Everything about him seemed perfect. His dress was perfect, his manners were impeccable and there didn't seem to be a dark thought in him. By the look of him, he was simply happy to be there with all his friends.

Maybe it was the idea of happiness that seemed so foreign. Dory wasn't sure she trusted it. At no point had she ever seen Vivian happy. Livinia was only happy when she wasn't stuck with her own company. Lady Pettifer was content. But Archie looked happy and bright. Dory watched as he leaned over and kissed his wife on the cheek. A rush of envy bubbled up and she pushed it down. Happiness should be encouraged in the world, not begrudged.

The group moved out onto the veranda, where the pool glittered enticingly. Again, Dory was struck with how far away she was from her station in life. Could she even describe this to her mother? Some of the things she'd experienced, she'd actually omitted from her mother's letters, fearing her mother warning her she was getting above herself. There was a hint in her mother's letters saying so. Their lifestyle was not hers, and she couldn't forget that.

Slowly, the group spilled down the sweeping stairs to the pool below, where a few of the girls sat down along the edge and cooled their legs. Dory stayed back. The truth was that she didn't connect with the girls. They tolerated her presence, but were never friendly beyond politeness. In saying that, they were never overtly unkind, which Dory was grateful for. But she suspected they took their cue from

Archie's behavior towards her. They were gracious because he was kind. If he was something other, they would be too.

There was a bar set up by the pool. "Champagne, Dory?" Archie called.

"That would be lovely," Dory answered. He brought over a bulbous glass with the bubbling, slight honey-colored liquid. Dory liked champagne. Before coming to the coast, she had only tasted it after her cousin's baptism. Here there was no occasion that didn't justify popping a cork. Maybe she was getting a little used to life above her station.

Two of the men grabbed racquets and headed across the lawn over the next few minutes, the whole group seemed to gravitate toward the courts. The tennis courts were down in elevation from the house, set amongst orange trees dotted with fruit that were still green. They provided lovely shade for anyone watching the game.

As Dory sat down on one of the benches a little away from the others, she watched Terry Wilcott. He had a very open face with slightly slanting eyes, giving him a perpetually bored look. If she had to guess, she would think he was around twenty-seven. Leather shoes were slightly scuffed as if he didn't care for them properly.

"Your inquisition is going gangbusters," Vivian said wryly. "So far you've only managed to hack a stammering hello to Archie. If you're going to play detective, you actually have to speak to people."

The urge to argue was flaring inside her, but she couldn't. "I just haven't got around to it."

"Too distracted watching Archie on the court?"

Pairs of men had taken to the court, the ball in sharp percussions between them. Archie was one of them. What was this incessant focus on Archie? Perhaps she had been watching him a little. Annoyingly, Vivian pounced on anything she did that indicated the remotest degree of interest, as if he were in cahoots with her mother to ensure she got no ideas above her station. Well, if Vivian was going to point it out, she wasn't going to cower. "I like Archie," she said pointedly. "He's a very kind man. I find kindness very compelling—intriguing. It makes you wonder about a person, who can afford to be so kind." For a moment, Dory felt a flare of panic, wondering if Vivian would from now point out how intriguing she found Archie every moment of the day. It would be utterly juvenile. She didn't, after all, have a crush on Archie. She just liked how kind he was, and how comfortable he seemed in his own skin. That was it—his self-assurance didn't seem put on, and that really was intriguing.

Vivian was silent for a moment, running his finger along the top lip of his glass. The liquid inside was brown, so he was obviously starting with liquor fairly early in the day. Whiskey, probably. He seemed to like whiskey.

"Don't confuse kindness for pity."

Dory's breath stopped in her chest. It was a cruel statement, maybe even the cruelest he'd imparted on her. Was it designed to erode any comfort she felt being there? It had to be designed to do something. She turned to him. "I think that's the point, Vivian. It isn't pity I feel from him, it's just a plain welcome without any underlying need to prove something."

"To prove what?"

"You tell me," she said, refusing to look away.

"All I am saying is that you're not going to prove a great detective if you are always cowering in a corner."

That wasn't what he had been saying at all, and they both knew it. Dory had faced him down and she'd won. She felt it in her bones. A lightness washed over her, but she didn't know exactly what or why.

His gaze lingered for a moment, then he looked away. "Terry, come here," he called and Terry looked up from across the other side of the tennis court. Getting up, he walked around until he reached them.

"Vivian," he said in acknowledgement as he reached them. "What's the urgency?"

"Miss Sparks here wishes to speak to you."

Surprise registered on Terry's face. "How can I help you, Miss Sparks?"

Drink in hand, Vivian walked away.

Chapter 15

Uncomfortably, Dory shifted in her seat.

"How can I help you, Miss Sparks?" Terry repeated.

"Uhmm," she started, not quite knowing how to proceed. She wasn't actually assisting a policeman here; she was doing this because she felt she needed to. "I was hoping you could tell me a little about Baron Drecsay," she said and noted his surprise. "Actually, Lady Pettifer has asked me to talk to you. She is well acquainted with his family." Hopefully that would give her some legitimacy in questioning people about this murder.

"He doesn't have any family," Terry stated.

"He has some relations in England."

"Only distantly."

Why did it matter, Dory wondered. "Yes."

With a sigh, he sat down on the bench next to her. "What do you want to know? I don't know who murdered him. Livinia was the one who found him, but I guess you've already spoken to her."

"Did he have any enemies?"

"I already told the police this."

"And from what we hear, they attributed guilt to some cuckolded husband, but no one has been arrested."

"Perhaps they're still gathering evidence."

Dory refused to be deterred, remembering how nothing would sway DI Ridley from his line of questioning. "Do you know who they suspect?"

Terry looked as if he was about to speak for a moment, but then paused. "I don't, actually."

"You were good friends."

With a shrug, Terry crossed his arms. "I suppose you could say so."

"And he didn't tell you about any married woman he was congressing with?"

"Congressing?" Terry said with a smile. "No, he didn't, but it wouldn't surprise me. Drecsay liked women, particularly since the countess' death. I suppose you heard about his relationship with Countess Tirau?"

"I understand she was very generous to him."

"I think the old bat liked to think someone like Drecsay was actually enamored with her. They're all like that, secretly, wanting to know young, handsome men find them fascinating. Granted, Drecsay could charm any girl out of her knickers, particularly rich ones."

"And he was interested in Livinia, wasn't he?"

"Livinia's a smashing girl. Anyone who manages to set a ring on her finger would be set, wouldn't they? Looks and money. Some would say that's a winning combination. Maybe Drecsay was trying his luck. I don't know; he didn't tell me. But I do know he was seeing some floozy on a regular basis—some French girl. Not the kind you build a future with, if you know what I mean."

"Charming," Dory said dryly.

Terry stood up. "Maybe something related to this girl is responsible."

Unlikely, thought Dory, as the murderer had been invited to Lady Tonbridge's party.

Turning back to her, Terry continued. "Just because he looked like a saint didn't mean he was one. In fact, he left a lot of people on the coast out of pocket. Not too careful with paying people back. Guess he didn't have to be. Countess Tirau eventually took care of everything after some pleading and earnest declarations of devotion." Terry snorted, then smiled. "The guy was a piece of work. You have to give him that. He was fun to know, provided you weren't stupid enough to line his pockets. The guy did as he pleased. It's not a surprise that someone offed him; it was bound to happen sooner or later. Maybe all the better for Livinia."

Picking a speck of dirt off his shirt, Terry gave her the slightest nod before walking away. Dory watched him go, and slip back amongst his friends.

What had she learned that was new? The account of Drecsay's character was consistent with what other people were saying, except for Livinia, who was obviously under the assault of this man's charm. Everyone said he had been charming. And again, the countess with their 'mutually beneficial' relationship. What was new, however, was the mention of a girl he was seeing, a French, local girl—a floozy, Terry had called her.

The way Terry had said it, Dory expected that this girl had been a feature in his life. Prince Barenoli hadn't mentioned her, but then Dory suspected there were plenty of things he hadn't mentioned. Perhaps she needed to go see him again, but she wasn't sure he would agree to a second meeting.

And who was this girl? Was she in some way responsible? The circumstances suggested not, but then she could well know more about what was going on in Dreesay's life around and prior to his murder. But how in the world was she supposed to find this girl? If she had his address book, things would be so much easier. No doubt, the police had it. Surely, they wouldn't be careless enough to overlook such a vital piece of evidence. Could she go and ask to see it? She could well imagine the unimpressed look from the inspector if she did.

Address book aside, the police would not have gathered everything, so his effects would still be somewhere—perhaps even at the hotel he was staying at. It wasn't far away.

A tennis ball flew past her, breaking Dory out of her concentration.

"Sorry, Miss Sparks," Richard said as he passed by her bench in search of the ball. A tight smile fleeted across her lips. The purpose of her visit to this party had been completed with her discussion with Terry—interview, it was in reality. Maybe she would even go so far as to call it an interrogation, she thought with a chuckle.

Now, she was stuck here for hours. Livinia and Vivian were not going to want to return home anytime soon and her coming along had been complicit with their schedules—not her own. Hours of this stretched in front of her. But then Nice was only a short drive away, wasn't it?

She could simply pop over and be back well before anyone wanted to go home.

The possibility of doing something useful sat brightly in her chest when she rose from her bench. She decided to tell Livinia instead of Vivian. It seemed her relationship with Vivian had reached a new low and she didn't want a second round of his jabs just at the moment.

"Livinia," she said lightly as she approached where Livinia sat with a group of girls around a table. Livinia looked over guardedly. It was obvious that Livinia was wary of being inclusive, no doubt finding Dory that bit 'not right' for her group of friends. "I thought I'd quickly pop over to Nice. Back in a tiff."

The expression on Livinia's face showed relief. Dory hadn't realized she was quite such a burden for Livinia, which made her want to escape this company more than ever.

"Alright. Have a good time," Livinia said, not even a bit curious as to why Dory would go to Nice.

Dory almost ran back up the stair toward the house. Meredith looked up as she reached the veranda, where she was arranging the table. There was going to be a meal at some point, Dory realized. "Need to pop out for a bit."

With a gracious smile, Meredith continued with her task. Dory wasn't sure she had ever felt quite so foreign here on the coast, and not foreign in the sense that she was from England, but foreign to the people who lived here. In a way, she told herself off for caring. DI Ridley wouldn't care. He had a job to do and she needed to approach things the same way. He certainly didn't have a crisis of identity every time he investigated a crime. Maybe it was time she grew a backbone and got on with the job.

Her sense of purpose renewed, she went to the car and started it. The engine rumbled to life and it whined as she backed up to make her way down to the coast road. The wind in her hair, she felt wonderful—a little like Vivian's judgment and persecution was lifted off her.

This trip to Drecsay's hotel could be a complete waste of time, but it could also provide some vital clues. In addition, she wondered what had happened to Drecsay himself, his body, she meant. Was he still here? According to Prince Barenoli, he had no family, so what had happened to the body? Had he been returned to Hungary? Was it even possible to return a body to Hungary? It could travel along Italy and Yugoslavia, she supposed. But if he had no family, who was to arrange his travel? Were his distant British family stepping in and offering to help? Nothing about that had been mentioned.

Chapter 16

The Hotel Carlone was a nice Victorian building, painted white with a wealthy display of windows. It was a little further along than the more extravagant hotels, such as where his friend, Prince Barenoli, was staying. Still, it was a respectable address.

Dory had parked right in front and made her way to the reception. A man with neat hair and a carefully preserved suit stood behind the wooden desk. "Mademoiselle," he said with a curt nod as she approached. His name was printed on a brass badge pinned to his lapel.

There were some people milling in the lobby. "I wonder, Monsieur Legrand, if we could speak in private about a delicate matter."

The man's eyebrows rose and so did his chin, so he was now looking down his nose at her. The disapproval wafted off him. Dory had no idea what he assumed that to mean, but it was something he was strictly disapproving off.

"Mademoiselle," he said indulgently, "I am a very busy man."

"Well, Baron Drecsay is not so busy these days and that is who I am here to speak about."

Further surprise pushed the man's eyebrows even higher. Then he frowned. "This way," he said, leading her toward a nondescript door, built to blend into the wood paneling behind the desk. It led to an office of good size. The furniture wasn't the latest, but it was well cared for, and he bid her to sit down by his desk. "How can I help you, Mademoiselle… "

"Sparks," she said. "I have been asked by Lady Pettifer, who is acting in the interest of Baron Drecsay's extended family, to see that poor Baron Drecsay is being properly cared for."

"Oh, would this Lady, or possibly his extended family members, wish to settle the poor baron's account with us?"

"That is a question to put to his estate, I think."

"Well, some of his creditors have already been here, by order of the local *magistrat*, may I add."

This was news to Dory and she must have shown it on her face.

"Some of his creditors came, claiming they had the right to his things in recompense for what he owed."

"They took his things?"

"Not everything. They left disappointed, I'm sure. The baron had some trinkets, but nothing of any real value. I am certain no one has had their accounts paid in full."

"So what is left?" Dory asked, disappointment flaring in her.

"Some toiletries. A rather nice silver comb. His clothes. Some books."

"No diaries or letters?"

"No. You can see the things if you wish. They are in a box."

It hadn't occurred to her that the baron's room had been packed away, but of course it had. A hotel couldn't afford to keep a room for a man who wasn't there to pay for it—or for previous nights, it seemed.

"Yes," Dory said, still battling with her disappointment. She'd felt so assured that some important clue would come out of this. The manager disappeared and returned with a cardboard box. It seemed too small to be the remains of a man's life.

The manager had been correct though, in that there was little inside—nothing that told her anything.

"No one has come for his belongings?" she asked after replacing the lid on his belongings. There really was nothing in there that would be of use.

"Only people seeking something to gain. Obviously people looking for more, because some of his things still have value—his clothes for example. Best quality, but his creditors were not interested."

"What did they take?"

"I did not see. Jewelry, perhaps."

"Was the baron a man who wore jewelry?"

"Obviously, he wore a signet ring. He had a gorgeous Cartier watch. A distinguished diamond tie pin as well." Dory got the feeling this man could describe the jewelry in detail. "But they were not here when he died." It seemed the manager had checked, and probably before anyone else had accessed the room. Dory would bet her arm there was other jewelry in his room that this man wasn't mentioning. The pieces he was describing would likely have been on the baron's person at the time he'd died, which meant the police had them. Dory hadn't noticed at the time and she chided herself. DI Ridley would probably have noticed, but she had been too shocked and distracted to observe such details.

"You never observed anyone act aggressively toward the baron?" she asked.

"No," the man said lightly as if it would never occur to him.

"I understand he was familiar with a local girl," Dory finally said.

The man stroked his chin absently. "Yes. Marie, I believe her name is. Chard."

"Did the police ask about her?"

"No, they were interested in the English women he was associated with. There was obviously the Countess Tirau. Their association was well known."

"What other English women did he know?"

"Sometimes he had women here. They came and went. He was a beautiful man. Usually, they didn't introduce themselves. Mostly Marie. Beautiful man, beautiful woman."

"Was she a lady of the night?" Dory asked lightly.

The man shrugged. "Who is to say?"

"Do you know where I can find her?"

"I don't know. Maybe she wishes not to be found."

With that, Dory sensed that the manager's interest and attention had run out, so she thanked him for his time, and wrote down the Beaulieu Villa number on a card and asked him to call if there was anything else he could think of.

Dory left the building and walked into the sunshine again. For some reason, the hotel manager's office had left her feeling a bit cold, which was unusual. She didn't really want to return to Archie Wilshire's house just yet. Kindness aside, she felt uniquely uncomfortable there, exasperated by Vivian's presence. Because of that, she was in no rush to get back, so she walked along the promenade along the edge of the gloriously turquoise blue water. Never had she seen water so bright before. It looked like a jewel.

On her walk, she recounted all the things she'd heard and knew. There were creditors who had come looking for his things. Marie Chard was undoubtedly his lover—the most consistent one, but not the only one. She could or could not be a prostitute according to Monsieur Legrand's reaction to her question. But if he was seeing her on a regular basis, and his friends knew about her, it suggested there was a relationship there.

It was unlikely Livinia knew about this woman. Dory couldn't imagine that she wouldn't care. Some men had mistresses as a given, but Dory couldn't see Livinia being a person who would tolerate that. Thinking back on it now, Dory realized she hadn't asked the manager if Drecsay's relationship with Marie superseded the death of Countess Tirau. Perhaps it didn't matter. If the countess disapproved of him seeing other women, it might be that he associated with one that would be below her regard.

It was a question she could probably put to Terry, but she wasn't sure if it mattered. Terry might know where to find this woman.

Returning to her motorcar, she turned around and headed along the coast again, trying to put order to all the questions she had. The next thing to do was to find this Marie. If she was in a relationship with him, she might know why he was killed, because no one else seemed to have a clue. It could even be that this woman was responsible, but then again, could she have snuck into a party and killed him? If she dressed the part, perhaps she could. Had she discovered that her lover was waiting for a pretty, rich heiress in a secluded spot and become enraged enough to kill him?

The butler would have kept an eye on anyone arriving at the party and he would have told the police if anyone unusual or uninvited had arrived. That would have informed their investigation into an entirely other direction, so Dory concluded there had been no unusual person attending the party. It meant she had to focus on the people who were at the party, which was almost everyone belonging to the British enclave on the coast.

To her annoyance, when she arrived back at the party, her parking spot had been taken by some new arrival while she had been gone and she had to find another quite far away. She was looking forward to returning here as much as she would a hole in the head, but she had a job to do.

The party had left the tennis court behind to languish along the veranda, elegantly draped over the equally elegant furniture. Terry was leaning against the wall, standing with drink in hand. His eyes were a little slower and more glossy, and he groaned as she approached. With a bit of drink in his belly, he was more honest about his feelings, not that he had particularly been holding back before.

Dory smiled tightly. "You mentioned that woman, Marie Chard. Do you know where I can find her?"

"God, what would you want to find her for?"

"Just to see what she has to say. She knew Baron Drecsay well. Perhaps he confided in her."

Terry performed an uncaring shrug. "I don't. I don't even know if she's around anymore. It was a while ago since I met her. Not the kind of girl who sticks around, if you know what I mean."

Truthfully, Dory didn't know what he meant, but she also didn't want to reveal her ignorance over what seemed a judgemental throwaway comment.

"Do you know where she was last?"

"I assume they spent most of their time together at his hotel. I wasn't privy to what they did in private. As for where she was when they weren't together, I have no idea."

He took a deep sip of his drink.

"Pretty, though," he said after a while. "The coast attracts pretty girls like flies, and they all want something. Attracted by title or money. They're all after something they don't have themselves."

This was hardly relevant. What was he telling her? Just spreading some form of bitterness? "And what was Marie after?"

"Perhaps she was hoping Drecsay would fall in love with her enough to marry her, give her some respectability. Who wouldn't want to be a baroness? If all other things were equal, wouldn't you?"

"All the barons I've met are miserable people," Dory said tartly. With the exception of perhaps Archie, and Lady Pettifer, of course, she hadn't met an upper-class twit she'd like to know better.

Terry found this inordinately amusing and he laughed. "Purport yourself uncorrupted by titles and wealth?" An edge of sarcasm laced his voice.

"I don't pretend to know myself enough to hazard a guess," Dory said dismissively, having no interest in getting into a discussion about her character with this man. Having dealt with Vivian before, she had no interest in entering some kind of discourse for this man to prove his own prejudices.

Chapter 17

Marie Chard proved difficult to find. She wasn't listed in the phone book, which wasn't perhaps surprising, because it was an expensive service and few could afford it. Trying to call the gendarmerie also proved fruitless and an exercise in absurd frustration, resulting in Dory being told that they could not be used as a meeting service.

With a groan, Dory hung up. She now had no idea how to find this woman. Terry had alluded that she could perhaps have left town, but then the hotel manager had clearly suggested she was a local girl, which meant she lived here somewhere.

If she had been a foreigner, she could easily go to the relevant consulate, who kept track of where everyone could be reached. Who knew it would prove so hard to find a person.

With a sigh, Dory rose from the small chair by the telephone table and walked back to the salon. "I'm afraid the gendarmerie were no help at all. I have no clue how to find this woman."

"Normally the right retailer could push you in the right direction, but I don't think this woman visited the retailers who keep records."

"Perhaps Prince Barenoli will know. I will send him a note later." Dory signed again. "We just don't seem to be getting anywhere. I was hoping Marie Chard would shed some light on why this man died. If there was anyone he would confide in, surely it was her."

"I'm afraid I don't know anyone who would be aware of this girl."

Feeling her spirits flag further, Dory sighed. "You figure this would be the most basic skill involved with investigating."

"We never claimed to be skilled," Lady Pettifer said, popping a candied almond in her mouth. "I wish I had bought some sherbets while we were in Nice."

"I will get some if I go there anytime soon, provided they haven't run out." Along with sugar, the supply of some luxury items were dwindling.

"Well, if we want to know what a professional would do in this instance, perhaps we should ask a professional," Lady Pettifer suggested.

"I tried that, but the inspector won't even speak to me."

"There is another one, though, who might be more willing to lend his ear and offer advice."

"Oh," Dory said. It hadn't occurred to her to ask DI Ridley for help. He may not be able to offer any direct assistance, but he could potentially tell her how to go about finding someone. "I will write to him."

A scrape sounded upstairs.

"Someone's risen," Lady Pettifer said.

Both Livinia and Vivian had returned early in the morning, being driven home by Richard. Livinia had put Dory out of her misery and urged her to drive home, saying they would find a way back without her. It had been a mercy and Dory had jumped at the chance. Now it was close to two in the afternoon and one of them was finally rising.

By the sounds of the steps, Dory knew it was Vivian, who appeared with his shirt open, displaying his white undershirt. "I will change," he said. "I'm just in dire need of something liquid."

"Good night, I take it," Lady Pettifer said.

"It did get a bit messy towards the end. Dory, here, didn't last the distance."

"Much too sensible," Lady Pettifer added.

Again Dory felt the weight of Vivian's judgment. Yesterday it had been for being there. Today his complaint was that she hadn't been there. Could he be so kind as to make up his mind? It seemed like he wanted to complain more than anything else.

"I will go write that letter," Dory said and stood.

"What letter?"

None of your concern, Dory wanted to say.

"We thought we'd ask that policeman back in England how we should proceed from here. We appear to need a little guidance."

Vivian was quiet for a moment. "Perhaps you shouldn't proceed. It could be that the police are not making further inquiries because they shouldn't."

"Or they are simply too busy and too uncaring that some foreigner has been dispatched. If he were a spy, it wasn't as if they are going to publicly acknowledge it." It seemed someone had been discussing the case with him, perhaps at the party last night.

"I really don't think that's the case," Lady Pettifer said.

"Someone at the Tonbridge's party killed him," Dory said and a silence descended. "So either one of the members of the illustrious British enclave is a spy hunter, or there is another reason altogether for this murder."

"It does seem unlikely that anyone would choose to take care of a spy in such a setting."

With a nod, Dory left the spot where she stood by the door and retreated to her room, where she could write her letter. In a way, she felt nervous. She'd had no communications with DI Ridley in any form since he had left Wallisford Hall. It could be that he'd ignore her letter completely. At the time, she had been of assistance to him, but she wasn't sure he would give her the time of day otherwise.

Sitting down at her desk, she pulled out a crisp sheet of paper and tried to think of what to write. Perhaps she should explain the situation first. With some false starts, she finally put her pen to the paper and started writing down what had happened and the things she had found out. What she really wanted to understand was what to do next. She paused. Maybe he would just tell her to leave it to the French police to deal with, like Vivian had—like everyone else was. Dory didn't know this man she was investigating—she didn't particularly like this man, but that was beside the point. Anyone deserved justice in such a situation. And there was a murderer here in this English society along the coast.

For a moment, she wondered if Vivian resented her for her part in uncovering his mother's deed. It was unlikely, but potentially possible that the woman would not have been found out if it hadn't been for Dory.

Still uncertain if she had written down the right things, or if she was even right in asking for guidance, she folded the letter and placed it in an envelope. She didn't know the exact address, so she wrote DI Ridley, Metropolitan Police, London. Surely the police would know how to direct it to the correct place.

Getting up from her seat, she returned downstairs to the salon with the letter in hand. To her relief, Vivian was no longer there. If Lady Pettifer noticed the tension between them, she didn't remark on it.

"Ah, have you written?"

Dory held up the letter.

"Excellent. Mr. Fernley," Lady Pettifer called and her butler appeared after a few moments. She did have a bell for calling him, but she usually bypassed it and simply asked for him. He seemed to hear her wherever he was. "Could you run down to the airport near Cannes and see if you can get this on this evening's flight.

"Yes, madame," he said and took the letter. Dory watched it leave the room and then as Mr. Fernley walked out to the car.

"It should be with him in a couple of days," Lady Pettifer said. "I wonder what he will tell us, but hopefully he will have some advice on how to find this woman. It must be a specialty of a policeman, determining how to find someone."

"I hope he writes back."

"Of course he'll write back. Why wouldn't he?"

"I am sure he's busy."

"It is in the nature of a policeman to assist."

Dory smiled. "Perhaps you are right." She couldn't help but wonder where he was and what he was doing. Was he solving some case somewhere? It could be that he wasn't in London at all, in which case the letter could take much longer to reach him.

"He was a lovely man, wasn't he?" Lady Pettifer said and Dory had to pull herself out of her thoughts.

"Yes," she said quietly.

"Completely unattached, as I recall. He would be perfect for you."

Color flared up Dory's cheeks. She wasn't normally one to get embarrassed about something like that—in fact, she wasn't normally one to swoon over any man, but she had liked DI Ridley. There was something very sensible about him. He also seemed to know exactly what to do when the occasion required it. Without a doubt, he was an excellent investigator, relentlessly pursuing the person responsible for the crime he was investigating.

All in all, Dory wasn't sure her interest in solving murders would have been left unexplored if she hadn't met him. In a way, perhaps she was trying to do what he did.

"Until we hear back, I think it's best we put the whole thing behind us," Lady Pettifer said. "Oh and now the tea is cold and we sent Mr. Fernley away."

"I'll refresh the pot," Dory said with a smile, knowing full well Lady Pettifer hoped she would do so the minute she'd said it.

Chapter 18

The next couple of days were spent trying to avoid Vivian. When he was at the house, she found herself in need of a long walk, returning when he had gone again, or she had been absent long enough. Her strategy didn't always work and he would be sitting either in the covered seating area outside or in the salon. Luckily, he seemed to ignore her much of the time as well. Still, Dory knew she could bear the brunt of his moods anytime he felt like it.

The sky was sunny and pure blue. A warm breeze was coming off the sea, but the house was starting to build up heat in the afternoons.

Today, both Vivian and Livinia were staying at home, which meant the house would likely feel crowded. It was by no means a small house. Perhaps Dory would see herself off to a secluded corner and read. It would be an evening of gin and tonics. Lady Pettifer always liked a gin on a hot day.

Walking into the house, the warm atmosphere felt repressive, and she wasn't in the mood to read. Surely, she couldn't go for another walk. She'd just returned from one and was hot and sweaty as a result. What she wanted was to cool down. The sea, she thought. Maybe a dip was exactly what she needed, so she went upstairs and dressed in the deep navy maillot she had bought in Cannes. It was lovely and it fit her perfectly. It had a rounded neckline and it finished at on her hips.

With towel over her shoulder and her book in hand, just in case, she left the house again, feeling a sense of purpose. The path down to the sea led through the extensive gardens along the rough terrains of the hillside, then down a rocky path to the small wooden jetty.

Spreading the towel on the jetty, she left everything there and climbed down the ladder into the refreshingly cool water. It had a sting of coldness for only a moment, then it mellowed into wonderful.

The water was so clear she could see all the rocks along the bottom and even some of the sea life. Diving under, all noise disappeared for a moment and she felt alone. The unpleasantness of the day was cleared away and she emerged tasting salt on her lips.

Glittering sun reflected all around her and she swam away from the jetty, where she turned around and floated for a moment. Swimming in the River Darent Lake had always been their summer outing as she'd grown up. They would cycle over and picnic by the lake shore. It had been the most marvelous days growing up—they'd been happy. Lower Darent Lake didn't have the spectacular colors of the Cote D'Azur, but it had its own charm, and Dory felt a pang of longing for home.

Gradually, the water started feeling cold and Dory swam back to the jetty and climbed out, laying herself down in the sun.

Baron Drecsay snuck into her mind. It felt wrong that he would never experience another day like this, just because someone had decided to steal his life from him. There had to be some way of moving ahead.

The sun quickly warmed her and she decided to return to the house before she started to burn. Unfortunately, her complexion wouldn't allow her to lie in the sun for very long and now had to seek shade.

The path to the house felt much steeper on the climb up, the breeze cooling her wet swimming costume as she walked through the shaded parts of the garden.

"Miss Dory," she heard Mr. Fernley call.

"I'm here," she called out.

"A phone call for you."

"Oh," she said and ran up the rest of the path and through the garden. Her towel was flung over her shoulder and she wrapped it around her as she approached the house.

The telephone was sitting on a small table in the hallway, the receiver lying on its side. Picking it up, she held it to her ear. "Hello?"

"Miss Sparks."

Dory recognized DI Ridley's voice immediately, even with the relentless crackling along the line. "DI Ridley. I didn't expect your call. I am so pleased to hear from you."

"I received your letter."

"Yes, I am sorry to bother you with this, but we seem to have stalled in our investigation. I know many feel we shouldn't, but the police here do not have the time to look particularly deeply into this."

"Much is being diverted everywhere," he said. It was hard to hear the exact intonation of his voice. "You mentioned the next step was to find this girlfriend, a local girl."

"Yes, but we struggle to find her. She is not of the community Lady Pettifer belongs to." She was going to add herself too, but it felt wrong in more than one way. "The police cannot assist us, so we do not know where to look."

"Census data is always a good place to seek people if you are looking for someone quite static, but it can be difficult to reach the census office if you are in a more rural location. You could call."

"Of course," Dory said, feeling slightly stupid because in hindsight, it was such an obvious avenue. "I should have thought of that."

"But most likely, if this girl is more of a goodtime girl, as you seemed to allude, just asking for her in some of the pubs is usually a quicker way of finding someone."

Dory didn't see any need to explain that the French didn't have pubs as such, but they did have taverns, and there were clubs and bars around where she could ask. Perhaps any of the drinking establishments near the Hotel Carlone. The baron and Marie were likely regular patrons there. It seemed so obvious now. How had she not thought of it? "I will ask in the establishments around the hotel where the baron lived."

"They might not provide you an answer, but if she was a local girl, then you could probably hone down on her district, then repeat until you get a street. From there it should be relatively simple to find her house, or her family's. If she has left town, her family will know where she is, and even how to reach her. Be careful, though. She might be the person responsible. And perpetrators do rash, irresponsible—even illogical—things when they are cornered. You shouldn't go alone."

"I won't. I promise."

"And I don't mean you and an elderly lady. Take someone who can guard you. It always pays to have someone watching your back."

"Yes, I will." Unsolicitous thoughts turned to Vivian, but she couldn't say he would actually agree. The thought of running around Nice with Vivian, looking for a trace of a woman seemed almost absurd.

"Typically with murder, the motives are primarily jealousy or money. Look to those first. Lady Wallisford didn't neatly fit into those, but most murders do."

Dory nodded even though he couldn't see her. "Thank you."

"You can write to me again if you wish, but it appears I will be at the Pirbright Camp in Surrey in the near future. If you write to the Met, there is a good chance it won't reach me."

"Pirbright?" she said.

"My letter to appear just arrived," he said a little more quietly.

"Oh," Dory said with surprise. "You're being conscripted."

"Effectively yes; technically it's not officially conscription. The expectation is clear. I head off in a couple of days."

"I see." She had no idea what to say to that. The pressure on people like him to join the struggle must be rampant. Was she supposed to send her condolences?

"Apparently they need men with certain skills."

"I hadn't realized," she repeated. The news still stunned her. "I hope you will be alright," she said without thinking.

"It's only training. I'm sure I will survive. Perhaps the French police are having the same issue with many of their officers being pressed into service."

That could explain why they seemed so unwilling to investigate the baron's murder. "I'm not sure England could do without its police."

"Not everyone is being called from the essential services. The firemen have all been exempt, but some of us investigators can be released, it seems."

At this point, Dory had no idea what to say. It felt as though she wanted to say so much, but couldn't think of anything appropriate.

"Are you safe where you are?" he finally asked.

"We seem to be. Lady Pettifer intends to stay put provided the Germans do."

It was silence down the line for a moment. "We should probably end this call."

"Yes, it must be costing you a bit. Thank you so much for your assistance. I know exactly what I need to do now."

There was a chuckle down the phone. "Goodbye, Dory."

Dory didn't want him to go. "I'll let you know how we progress."

"I would appreciate that."

With that, he hung up and the line clicked a few more times as the operators disengaged the calls, until Dory's phone was left with only static silence and she replaced the receiver.

Chapter 19

Dory felt a little stunned as she walked back to the salon, where Lady Pettifer, Vivian and Livinia were all sitting. They all turned to her expectantly, having heard her speaking on the phone.

"It was DI Ridley," she said absently. "He had some good advice."

"So you know how to proceed now?"

Dory sat down, eventually remembering that a question had been put to her. "Yes."

"You seem a bit startled."

"It was just… DI Ridley said he'd been asked to join the services and he was leaving his post."

"Everyone and their dog have been conscripted," Vivian said dismissively and all turned to him. "It's not unusual. Anyone with a hint of education is being conscripted into officer training."

"You have education," Livinia said.

"So I have. Knew it would lead to no good."

"You haven't received a letter, have you?"

"Turns out I have. Wasn't there to receive it, though. Had already left."

The room was silent for a moment.

"Like I said, everyone and their dog. Women too, apparently."

"What?!" Livinia said.

"Mostly nurses and eminently sensible girls, so I think you're safe, Livinia."

"Technically, I don't think women can be required to serve," Lady Pettifer said.

"Not if Sir Beveridge has his way. He seeks to conscript every woman in the country."

"I couldn't possibly go to war," Livinia piped shrilly.

"Don't worry, Livinia," Vivian said. "No one would subject the Germans to you. More likely they will send you to a farm to milk cows or something."

The horror on Livinia's face made Dory chuckle. It wasn't really funny, though. This only showed that the people in power didn't expect that the lack of aggression that had kept things peaceful would continue. And it seemed they could all be a part of the war. This thing that had seemed too abstract and removed had shifted closer. People she knew were being sucked into what she saw as a menacing cloud.

Everyone knew the losses that had occurred with the Great War. A whole generation of men had been lost. With men going to war, the chances of them not returning were high.

Absently Dory stroked her fingers along her mouth.

"Andrew," Lady Pettifer said and rose, marching over to the telephone. In a sense, it felt as though hearing of Andrew's conscription would be worse, because Lady Pettifer was a mother. As much as everyone worried about friends and acquaintances, mothers must be devastated.

This conversation and Lady Pettifer's reaction wasn't something Dory wanted to be a part of. Lady

Pettifer wouldn't want it either if it turned out Andrew, her son, had been conscripted. She bore blows in solitude.

"I have to go to Nice," Dory said.

"God, yes, let's get out of here," Livinia said. "All this talk of war makes my skin crawl."

With worry, Dory pressed her lips together, wondering if she should ask Vivian to accompany her. Livinia would be more of a hindrance if there was danger around. But she had no idea if Vivian would be of any use either. Use or not, anyone with ill intent would pause at taking on three people, even if they were essentially useless and oblivious.

Not that it mattered yet. Dory hadn't even located Marie Chard. When it came time to question, perhaps she would ask both of them to accompany her.

"He has received a letter, too," Lady Pettifer said at the door with a strained and tired voice. "I think I will rest for a while."

"In that case, we might continue with our inquiries," Dory said and stood. "Follow up on some of DI Ridley's suggestions."

With a nod, Lady Pettifer turned and walked toward the stairs. Sighing at the sight of Lady Pettifer's silent suffering, Dory felt awful. In a sense, it was hard not to think of it as a death sentence. Or at least Lady Pettifer would, who so remembered the telegrams relentlessly coming with dreadful news.

Without a son or a husband, Dory wouldn't receive such news, and her brothers were yet too young. If the war stretched on for four years like the Great War, then at least one would be pulled into the malaise as well. She couldn't imagine losing either of her brothers.

Maybe the fact that nothing had really happened yet meant there was still hope of a diplomatic solution. It could be that all of this ended without great loss. Surely no one wanted another war like the one before. It had devastated everyone.

"Come on," Vivian said. "I'll drive."

Still feeling deflated, Dory grabbed her hat off the coat stand. Livinia disappeared upstairs to change, leaving Dory and Vivian to stand by the car. An awkward silence hung between them.

"I am sorry to hear you have been conscripted."

"Wouldn't have happened if I'd been stupid enough to start a parliamentary career like Cedric."

"He's exempt?"

"All parliamentarians are."

Livinia finally appeared and they all got into the motorcar. Dory sat in the back, still feeling heavy from the day's developments. She spent most of the trip lost in her own thoughts while Vivian and Livinia chatted between themselves. Notably, since Vivian had arrived, they hadn't engaged in the petty barbs they used to sling at each other when she'd first met them. His jabs seemed to be exclusively reserved for Dory now.

The drive took long, but happened along beautiful vistas. The coastline was stunning the entire drive from St. Tropez, through multiple small villages and through Cannes.

"Why are you going to Nice, anyway?" Vivian asked.

"I'm going to ask around some of the bars if they know this Marie Chard woman." In a way, the murder seemed like a paltry concern against the looming specter of war, but that was exactly why they couldn't lose focus. Justice was still needed for this man.

Arriving in Nice, Dory asked Vivian to pull over by the Hotel Carlone, where she got out. "I'll meet you back here in two hours," she said.

"And what if we want to stay for more than two hours?" Vivian challenged.

For a moment, Dory was stumped. "Then I suppose I will take the bus." The bus was slow, but it did wind its way back along the coast. By no means was it a comfortable ride, but it would give everyone the flexibility to do as they wished.

"Two hours it is, then," he said before suddenly driving off.

With raised eyebrows, Dory simply watched them as they disappeared down the street, then decided she couldn't be bothered with Vivian and his strange behavior. She had a job to do.

Turning around, she spotted a brasserie. The baron and his girl must have visited there on a number of occasions. It was a nice place with beautiful standing lights between neat rows of wooden tables. The place had a warm, welcoming feeling.

A sharp-featured man stood outside in his starched white apron. It was that quiet period between lunch and supper, when many of the French took their siesta. "Monsieur," Dory said as she approached.

"Are you dining with us, mademoiselle?" he asked with a curt bow.

"No, I'm afraid not. I was wondering if you could assist me to find a woman that I believe frequented here with Baron Drecsay."

The man mused for a moment and Dory feared he would be as unhelpful as the manager at the hotel. "Baron Drecsay had many dining companions."

"I meant specifically Marie Chard."

"Oh, Marie. We have not seen her for a while. The baron met with an unfortunate fate, you know."

"I heard. It is just that his family wishes to give a gift to Marie, but they cannot find her." Dory was lying through her teeth, but she had to do something to get past the suspicion in the man's eyes.

"I see. I can tell her if she comes," he said with a shrug. "And you are?"

"Miss Dory Sparks. I am actually trying to track her down. Do you know where I could ask next?"

"I cannot help you. I don't know her address."

"I understand she is a local girl. Do you know the district she is from?"

"I believe Riquier."

That was quite far away. She would have to take the tram. "Perhaps I will try to find her there."

The maitre'd had lost interest and Dory thanked him before leaving. Riquier was a district she didn't know well, it was known for dense houses and the location of many of the tradesmen in the city. It wasn't a tiny place, but Dory knew it was the kind of neighborhood where the people knew each other.

One of the tram lines would take her straight there and she could relax for a moment and simply watch the busy streets of Nice pass her by. They were busy, but there did seem to be fewer people than the last time she had visited, which was only a week or so back. More people had to be leaving. Dory wondered if Lady Summernot and her sister had managed to find passage out.

Maybe it was time to broach the topic with Lady Pettifer as well. The emptying streets were alarming to see. It felt as though the whole world was anticipating something terrible.

Chapter 20

Marie proved not that hard to find. Dory asked a few vendors and eventually she was led to a second story apartment above a pharmacy. Marie lived with her mother in a small apartment and seeing it, Dory wished the baron's family actually had something for her. Although the chances that they would give any consideration to a girl like Marie were low.

Dory smiled as they sat down in the apartment's tiny reception room. The furniture was old and worn, but well serviced.

"I am trying to find out what happened to Baron Drecsay," she explained as Marie and her mother waited expectantly with their hands in their laps. Marie was very pretty with dark hair and lovely eyes. It wasn't a wonder she had caught the baron's eye. "I have not been able to find any enemies. But I think you know him better, and I was hoping you could set me on the right path."

"You wish to find who killed him? It wasn't me."

The police must have given her a hard time, Dory presumed. She would be the logical suspect. Ridley had told her to look for jealousy or greed first. "Did you observe any specific jealousy amongst his friends?"

"Nothing he was worried about. He liked to have friends of higher position than himself." It had to be Prince Barenoli she was referring to.

"There are some that say that Baron Drecsay was a spy."

Marie laughed. "No, he hated the Germans. Probably they say that because he was friends with Barenoli. Barenoli is only here because he cannot go home. Neither of them are spies. Only stupid people think that. Besides, Drecsay… he didn't like to do difficult things. He liked the easy life. He gets that woman to pay for everything."

"You mean Countess Tirau."

"Stupid woman." There was definitely a hint of jealousy there—or was it resentment.

"But with her death, her support ended. Did he inherit anything from her?"

"No, she gave him nothing!" Marie sounded offended. "All the work he did whispering compliments in her ear and she gave him nothing."

"One of his friends said he had some scheme to rebuild his family wealth. Did he say anything to you?"

"He always had ideas. He spoke of ideas, but he never did anything. Too lazy."

Dory had to wonder if Marie had even liked him. Or was she as dependent on him as he was on Countess Tirau? Did none of these people have the wherewithal to stand on their own feet and have true relationships? With a shake of her head, Dory dismissed the thought. Her judgment wasn't serving her at this moment. "I understood the countess was very generous, at times."

"Every once in a while, she would do what Drecsay wanted. Gifts here and there. Jewelry."

"Anything of note?"

"She gave him a car. Some land to build a house."

"She gave him land?"

"Yes, down in Antibes. Not good land. Average land."

"Do you think anyone would kill him for this land?"

"It was nothing more than farm land. I don't know. When I went, it wasn't much. Mr. Henri can tell you more."

"And who is Mr. Henri?"

"He is the countess' *advokat*."

"Her solicitor? Do you know where I can find him?"

Marie shrugged. "I never met him."

They talked some more, but Dory wasn't getting anything else that resembled a motive. Marie, as it turned out, didn't like Prince Barenoli, but he was rich, the woman pointed out. That forgave him a great deal, Dory assumed. Neither did she like Terry. He drank too much and was handsy. There were also other friends. Drecsay had a lot of friends.

When Dory brought up the subject of Livinia, Marie's face darkened and she called her a stupid English girl. Well, there was certainly jealousy there. It just wasn't directed at Drecsay, even though Marie's anger probably should have been. Women did tend to blame the other woman instead of the man who was inflicting the damage— as if they were incapable of taking responsibility for their own actions. But Marie had never met Livinia, or even knew what she looked like.

There seemed to be nothing else Marie could tell her. Drecsay liked to drink, liked to be the life of the party. And he had enjoyed his time after the countess' control had finished, but his finances had dwindled. Still, he hadn't seemed overly worried.

Bidding goodbye, Dory left, her mind mulling over the things that Marie had said. She painted the picture of a young man who cared little for consequences. In saying that, it seemed Drecsay had turned his attention to marriage and was seeking the most profitable return from it. Livinia had obviously been a target, and for someone like him, it would have been a good step.

Dory shuddered trying to imagine the life they would have—living here on the coast, slowly burning through Livinia's inheritance. Sadly, it wasn't a fate that would unduly disturb Livinia. She, too, would be happy to be the life of the party here on the coast—until the money ran out. But for her, perhaps the money would never entirely run out. She had her own Countess Tirau in her father.

It was a fate that Lady Pettifer would deeply disapprove of, but it was questionable how much control she had over Livinia. Livinia was a young woman of age. It wasn't as if anyone could blatantly tell her what to do. Maybe Marie was right and she was a woman bound to make stupid decisions. Drecsay was no longer in the picture, so perhaps there was hope for her to settle into a good marriage with a half-decent man. Some girls seemed allergic to decent men, though.

The tram took her back to where she had started outside the Hotel Carlone. Right on time, Vivian showed up sans Livinia.

"Livinia is staying," he said, waiting for Dory to get in.

"You didn't feel like staying yourself?"

He didn't answer her question. "So what did you discover in your investigations?"

"It seems Drecsay was looking for an heiress and had his sights on Livinia."

Dory could see the muscle in Vivian's cheek working. He did not like hearing that. If he had been around, Dory had to concede he would have had motive for murder. He'd been nowhere near, otherwise, Dory would have to suspect him again, like she had for the other murder investigation she had been a part of.

"Apparently the countess had given him some land down by Antibes. The girl said it wasn't particularly valuable land, but enough for him to build a house on."

"Land isn't hard to get around here."

"No, I suppose not," Dory admitted.

"Hard to think anyone would murder for a bit of land."

"People have killed for less. I suppose it depends on who inherits the land."

"Some distant relative in Hungary, no doubt. Whoever has inherited the title. So if you find some mysterious Hungarian hanging around, then you might have your man. Someone who would come all the way here to dispatch of a penniless baron for a worthless piece of land."

In Vivian's book, the land might be worthless, but he lived on an entirely different scale from most people. To someone like Marie, that land would be a fortune, even if she hadn't been impressed by it when she'd visited with Drecsay. Like Drecsay with his countess, Marie would inherit nothing from Drecsay. It could be said that she had lost more than anyone out of his death.

Vivian drove, his attention on the road. The sun was setting, painting glorious colors on the horizon. Again, Dory was struck with how beautiful it all was. But it was also starting to feel like an illusion, a distraction. "There were fewer people in Nice than the last time we visited."

"People are leaving," he said, but didn't elaborate further.

"What are you going to do about your conscription?"

For a moment, he looked over at her, then back at the road. "Well, I can't hang out here forever. Sooner or later, I will have to go back."

"Some would say that you could stay here and avoid it."

"Not if I ever want to show my face in society again," he said. Dory hadn't realized there would be such pressure. Ridley had alluded to it as well. "People are scrambling for excuses for their sons not to go, but deride others for it. It is the very height of hypocrisy. None of us are true conscientious objectors—we just object to our family members being called to serve."

They drove in silence for a while. This war seemed to be steamrolling ahead, unable and unwilling to take a moment to pause and reflect. "Is there any going back now?" she asked.

"It would be a miracle."

Mischief in St. Tropez

Chapter 21

"It would be hard to see how some farmland in Antibes would be a motive for murder," Lady Pettifer said as they sat in the dark around the dining table, lit only with candles. Livinia had not returned, and was in the bosom of her social circle for the night. Dory still didn't understand why Vivian had returned home. Perhaps he'd had enough. It could be that he didn't particularly enjoy the company of what was effectively Livinia's friends. They were a bit younger, perhaps.

"It would be truly something desperate."

"I will try to call this Mr. Henri," Dory said. "By the name, it is hard to tell whether he is English or French."

"Perhaps the countess' family can shed some light. I don't exactly know how to reach them." Lady Pettifer looked ponderous. "It wouldn't be something that her friends and acquaintances would know."

"Maybe I should try to reach Inspector Moreau," Dory said with a notion of dread. The inspector seemed less than willing to speak to her. "It's worth a try."

"Try it in the morning. We should be quite insistent. If they prove difficult, I could ask Major Dodds to call him."

"Who's Dodds," Vivian asked.

"The British consul in Nice. He can put a bit of pressure on the French authorities if we need him to."

"Useful," Vivan said. He looked bored as he sat and nursed his wine, or it could be the candlelight that displayed him so. Dory had to wonder if something had happened, or if it was the conscription that weighed heavily on him. That would be understandable. Dory couldn't even imagine what it would feel like to receive such a letter, to be forced to go off to war.

Earlier in the day, he had mentioned that they were recruiting educated men to be officers, which meant him. It was hard to imagine him as someone in charge of a platoon of men. Dory wasn't sure that was the right term, but Vivian would be directing men in the war effort. And Ridley. Ridley seemed more of a natural choice. He had directed men before, but what skills did Vivian really have?

Putting the uncomfortable thoughts away, she returned her mind to Drecsay, which seemed less confrontational to think about. There was no hint of a culprit yet, but the land was a lead she felt they needed to follow.

"Shall we listen to the news?" Lady Pettifer said and rose. "I could use a sherry, I think. Dory, would you like one?"

"I could handle a small one," Dory replied. After all this time with Lady Pettifer, Dory had learned to enjoy a sherry. Initially, it hadn't agreed with her, but over time, her appetite had learned to crave some after supper.

"Mr. Fernley, would you be so good as to turn on the wireless."

The man moved to do so and sharp static invaded their ears for a moment. The remnants of some melody played its last cords. They had made it just in time.

This is the BBC from London, the disembodied voice said gravely. *These are today's main events. Germany* has invaded Luxembourg, Belgium and the Netherlands. Both houses of Parliament have been summoned at six o'clock this evening, and the cabinet has met from eleven this morning to prepare our response. The French Parliament has also been meeting today. What news there is comes chiefly from broadcasting stations in Luxembourg City, Amsterdam and Brussels.

They all exchanged concerned looks, but no one spoke. They had been driving around Nice today and no one had been the wiser that Germany was marching across Europe toward them.

Allied troops are preparing their response, and so are our forces in Lille, both mobilizing to meet the Germans.

"It is starting," Lady Pettifer said, her voice completely toneless.

"Our troops will beat them back," Vivian stated. Dory could see the concern in his eyes. She'd actually never seen him truly concerned before.

The presenter went onto detail the resistance being put up in each of the countries to the invading army.

"They're invading three countries at once," Dory said, still not believing what she was hearing. "There wasn't so much as a peep when we were in Nice. It was just a normal day." She knew full well she was babbling, but she didn't know what else to do with the fear that bubbled up inside her. The Germans were invading, taking the small countries before they marched through to France. Would the French really stop them, like Vivian had asserted? Dory hoped so.

"Turn it off, Mr. Fernley," Lady Pettifer said. The silence was jarring and no one spoke.

"We have to leave," Vivian said after a while.

"I thought you said the French would hold them," Dory asserted.

"When have the French ever held anything. We have to leave. Getting rid of the landed gentry was the first thing the Germans did when they invaded Poland."

Lady Pettifer grimaced. "It is very worrying that the Germans seem to be attacking the civilian population. Very worrying indeed. But all this is happening up north. If not the French, then our troops will beat them back. It is all far away from here."

Vivian rose sharply and paced. Everyone seemed to be saying one thing and then the opposite.

"I might get some fresh air," Dory said and rose herself. Tears were forming in her eyes and she needed some time alone to deal with the emotions that were running away with her. So she walked out into the darkness of the garden outside. The moon was out and lit the landscape around her. It was utterly silent as if the coastline itself didn't care what the stupid people milling on its surface was doing. She felt stupid—on behalf of people in general, she felt stupid. This was a stupid thing to do—war, what use could it possibly serve. It would cause wholesale misery to everyone and for that?

Breathing rapidly, Dory had to slow down or she would start to hyperventilate. Her hopes had been that they would sort this—that it was all posturing and they would sort themselves out. Stupid people were leading them into war, and now they would all suffer. Life as Dory had known it was ending and something awful was going to take its place. Their lovely lives here on the coast could not continue. They had to leave.

Everything had seemed so distant before, but now the ugliness that had been brewing was chasing them away. It was even forcing Ridley and Vivian into the very war itself.

Coming across a bench, she sat down and stared out at the calm sea. Why did everything have to end?

She sat for ages, unable to deal with other people right now, or commiserate with their worry and concern. Too many worries circled around her own heart to have room for the concerns of others. In a sense, she was holding herself back from blind panic and couldn't afford to let anyone test her resolve.

After a long while, she saw headlights snake along the coast road in the distance. Did they know what had happened? Had their life effectively been torn apart too? Or were they blissfully unaware? Just a short while ago, Dory had been blissfully unaware.

Eventually the motorcar drew closer and Dory saw it veer in. It was coming this way. It had to be Livinia. She must have heard. Were the glittering party things in Cannes also panicking?

It really was time to head back, and Dory forced herself to rise. Suddenly, she felt exhausted. It was as though she had used up all her emotions at once and was now left completely empty.

The headlights of Livinia's motorcar, probably Richard's, swung around the tree as it pulled up next to the house.

"Have you heard?" Livinia's voice demanded inside the house. "It's unbelievable. I don't understand. This fucking war! They ruin everything."

Livinia's tirade wasn't far off what Dory was feeling.

"Everyone is shocked," Richard's voice came. "No one knows what to do. There's talk of midnight escapades across the country. They say we should pack up this minute and just drive north or west."

"It serves no one to head off like a headless chook," Lady Pettifer said. "In the morning, we will call Major Dodds and see what he says. We must be orderly with this."

Richard cleared his throat and sat down. "They say the Duke and Duchess left their lunch half eaten and fled earlier today. They must have been told before the announcement on the news. They just left everything and fled."

"Not a word," Livinia said. "They could have warned the rest of us."

"Perhaps they wanted clear roads for their escape," Vivian said and lit a cigarette. His panic had clearly subsided, and he was more or less back to his usual caustic self. Dory had to admire his resilience. "I bet they don't half admire Herr Hitler so much now."

"They were trying to avoid a war," Livinia said in anger. "Maybe if they hadn't been thrown out, they would have succeeded."

"Children," Lady Pettifer said. "We need cool minds. Tomorrow we'll call the consulate and plan what we are to do."

Chapter 22

At no point that night did Dory sleep. It was almost as if she didn't trust the wall to stand if she so much as closed her eyes. It was still unbelievable to think the Germans were marching toward them. It was impossible to imagine what this would entail. No doubt they were going back to England, but it would be an England at war, and Dory had no idea what that meant.

It was a given that she would return to England at some point; she just hadn't anticipated that it would be under these circumstances, which seemed unbelievable even as the war hadn't exactly cropped up overnight. She had always had that hope that it would fizzle to nothing.

With groggy eyes, Dory met the next morning. Her head ached and she felt awful. When she reached the salon downstairs, it seemed Lady Pettifer's night had been similar. "Terrible sleep," the woman said.

"Me, too," Dory confessed.

"It seems we must find some way of leaving here. There are still so many people on the coast. How are we all going to make our way back to the UK?"

"I don't envy the task that has befallen Major Dodds. You don't think he would simply leave us, do you?"

"It would be cowardly if he did," Lady Pettifer said with distaste. "I think he will do his best. He seems a sensible man."

"You know him."

"Well enough. It seems as our options reduced, traveling home seemed too difficult to deal with, and now we are in the lurch."

"I don't think flying is an option."

"There are too many of us here for it to be the strategy he will choose. The government will have to help us."

"And if they don't?" Dory asked.

"Then we will be in trouble indeed. I still think it will be a long time before the Germans make it all the way down here. The Italians are more of a concern, but so far, they have shown little indication that they want to participate. I don't trust that, though. It is well known that Mussolini dreams of restoring some semblance of the old Roman Empire."

"Well, he will have to compete with the Nazis and their empire," Dory said with distaste.

"I think for the time being, we are safe. We have time at the very least."

Lady Pettifer checked her watch, a bejeweled timepiece that Dory knew she had received from her late husband. "Perhaps I should call Major Dodds now." On painful knees, she rose from her seat and walked over to the telephone in the hall, speaking in French to the operator, who apparently couldn't put her through.

Before long, Lady Pettifer returned to her seat. "There is a queue to access his line," she said. "It seems every person on the coast is having the same idea."

A noise in the hall showed that someone else had risen, and Vivian appeared with his washed hair slicked back from his face. He looked like he had slept at least. "I'm starving," he said.

"Then we shall eat," Lady Pettifer said, and called for Mr. Fernley. "I suppose Livinia won't rise for a while. I understand Richard left early this morning."

Dory had heard a car start and drive away some time well before dawn.

It was going to be a hot day. Heat was already starting to build up. They walked into the dining room and sat down. It would take a few minutes before Mr. Fernley appeared with ham and eggs. Dory's body seemed to crave energy today.

"I think we should wait until tomorrow and then go to the consulate in Nice. It will be utter chaos today, so no need to add to it."

Vivian looked distracted with a deep frown marring his features. "I am going back to Switzerland," he said after a while.

"Vivian, you can't."

"I have to go collect Mother before it's too late."

"The Germans could have invaded by the time you get there. It's not worth the risk."

"If they invade, Mother would be exposed. Centuries past a noble could be assured of good treatment, but that is no longer the case. These Germans would as readily kill anyone with a title."

"I'm sure it is not that severe," Lady Pettifer said.

"Well, I am going shortly. I will collect her and… "

"And then what? She cannot come back to the United Kingdom. Technically, there is still a warrant out for her arrest and if she is arrested, she will hang."

"I know that," Vivian said curtly. "I will have to figure out what to do. Maybe Spain."

"To live under the rule of another insane dictator with dreams of an empire? Who knows what his role is going to be in all this? If he joins with the Nazis, which he could at any point, then things will be very dire indeed."

"The French wouldn't have a chance," Vivian said.

Dory simply looked from one to the other, too afraid to speak in case voicing her thoughts made them real.

"You need to get off the continent," Lady Pettifer said.

"Perhaps we'll go to Algeria or Morocco."

Concern shone through Lady Pettifer's eyes, but even Dory knew that Vivian wasn't changing his mind. As awful as Lady Wallisford was, she was still his mother, and Dory could sympathize with him wanting to fetch her. She would likely do the same if the positions were reversed.

Their food arrived and Dory struggled with her appetite, but she forced herself to eat. A few days ago, her main concern had been the lack of sugar, and now they were all being driven in different directions in desperate flight.

Livinia appeared through the door wearing her sunglasses. "I feel awful. I was hoping I would wake up today and it had all been a bad dream. Where's Richard?"

"He left early this morning," Lady Pettifer said.

"I can't believe he just left without a word. What if we needed him?"

"I guess at times like this, you see who people really are," Vivian said.

"That's unfair."

A silence descended as no one really felt like getting into an extended argument.

"What's going to happen to Mother?" Livinia said.

"Vivian has decided to fetch her," Dory said.

"And then you'll bring her here?" Livinia said hopefully.

"I don't know," Vivian replied noncommittally. "I don't know what options will be open to us. It might be better to head down to Italy. The Italian ports are still open. We could potentially get passage south."

"South?"

"Well, I can't bring her back to England, can I?"

"I'm sure they will make an exception considering the circumstances."

"And will you risk her life on that assumption?"

If Dory didn't feel that capital punishment was gruesome and unnecessary, she would be open to Lady Wallisford meeting the justice she deserved, but she couldn't bring herself to wish someone to hang.

"I will work something out," Vivian said after a while. "There are options."

"There has to be panic all over the country," Lady Pettifer said. "Everyone in the north must be heading south. The poor Belgians. They must be running like rabbits."

"Well, if they ever invade us," Vivian said. "There is nowhere to go."

"Except America," Livinia said.

"If things go very badly, maybe the next time we see each other, it will be in New York."

"Or the Bahamas."

"Not sure the Bahamas can take half the population of the United Kingdom descending on it," Lady Pettifer said. "In saying that though, I am sure Lady Ridgemont will be able to put us up in that villa of hers."

"Along with everyone else she knows."

"Why did we never invest in a villa in the Bahamas?" Lady Pettifer said furtively.

"Because you fell in love with the Cote D'Azur," Vivian pointed out.

"Yes," Lady Pettifer said absently. "Could you imagine traveling across the Atlantic every year?"

The conversation drifted to silence, and shortly after eating, Vivian went upstairs to pack.

"Is he going now?" Livinia asked.

"Yes, I think it is better he goes as soon as possible."

It didn't take him long to return, carrying a leather bag. They all gathered in the hallway.

"If the Germans invade Switzerland, you can't go."

It frustrated Lady Pettifer that Vivian didn't answer, instead kissed her on the cheek. He gave Dory an awkward kiss to, which would probably never have happened if it wasn't for the extreme circumstances. "Get them home," he said quietly so only she could hear. He was placing the task on her to ensure they got home. Dory nodded.

Then he walked outside and placed his bag on the backseat of his motorcar. Livinia followed him and they embraced tightly. That was an affection she hadn't really seen between the twins before. When it came down to it, it ran deeper than either of them let on.

Then he got in and drove without looking back. Not one for long-winded goodbyes. Livinia stood and watched for a while.

An anxious groan escaped Lady Pettifer. "He isn't a stupid boy," she said to reassure herself. "He will know how to watch out for danger."

Will he, Dory wanted to say. As far as she knew, Vivian had a strong sense of entitlement and a puffed-up sense of importance in the world. Hopefully those things would not lead him into trouble.

Chapter 23

The difference in Nice was stark. The streets were empty. They weren't really. People were hurrying along, but at first glance, they looked deserted. There was no one wandering leisurely down the promenade and the cafés were largely empty. Overnight, the world had changed.

Dory drove along the promenade until they reached the building where the consulate was. If there was any question as to where the people had gone, it appeared to be here. A crowd of people stood in a group outside the building, milling and chatting. There were grave expressions of worry on people's faces.

Pulling over, Lady Pettifer and Livinia got out. There were no available parking spaces so Dory had to keep driving down the road to find somewhere. It seemed people had driven from all around to reach the now swamped consulate. Dory doubted they would get much assistance today. Perhaps it had been a mistake coming here, but what else could they do? Hopefully the British Government had some plan for the people here on the coast. Surely they couldn't all be left to their own devices. There were a great many people here without the means of leaving on their own account.

A new set of worry descended on Dory. What would they do if they had to find their own way back? Perhaps Vivian was right and Italy was the best route, but heading into an uncomfortably fascist regime sat badly.

Their choices were Italy, Spain, or to find their way north to the Atlantic coast, or even closer to the fighting on the channel coast.

A parking space was available and Dory pulled in. It was a hot day and she could feel the heat of the ground through the soles of her shoes as she walked back toward the consulate.

A lone figure sat along the tables of a café she was approaching, all other tables empty. He was smoking and as Dory came closer, she saw that it was Prince Barenoli. A small coffee cup sat next to him.

"Your highness," Dory said and stopped.

"Miss Sparks," he said as he looked her over. It wasn't a lecherous look, more disapproving of what she was wearing. Dory smiled tightly.

"Going about life as normal despite what's happened?" she asked.

He shrugged and took a drag of his cigarette. "What point is there in panicking?"

"You're not scrambling to leave, then?"

"I have nowhere to go," he said, pulling a piece of tobacco off his tongue. "No one wants an Italian aristocrat."

"The Italians are not a part of this war."

"Not yet, but they will be."

"Do you really think so?"

"Mussolini is too greedy to stand back and watch the Germans claim all the spoils."

The Prince apparently believed the Germans weren't going to be stopped at the border. "So what are you going to do?"

With a shift of his head, he regarded her. "I don't know. Maybe I will go to Spain."

"Some have suggested Algiers," Dory said.

"Maybe that is a good place to wait out this madness."

"What do you know of the land down in Antibes that the Countess Tirau had bought for Baron Drecsay?"

"Even with a war, you do not give up?" he said with a chuckle. He took a drag and regarded her. "It is not worth much."

"Would anyone kill him for it?"

"I suppose it would be worth a few francs to the desperate. It was a joke, I think, on behalf of the countess. Drecsay wanted to build a home and she gave him awful land for it. She had a habit of buying him useless things. It amused her. It wasn't the only useless thing she'd bought him. She even bought him a small Scottish Island once, which I believe is probably the most uninhabitable place in the world. There were others, the more useless, the better. But this property was the first one in an accessible place, I suppose. Maybe that made it all the more vexing."

"So he was never going to build in Antibes?"

"I think he was—maybe just to spite her. But in the end, he had no money to. But a plump, little heiress would take care of that, no?"

He had to be referring to Livina's wealth, because she was certainly not plump in any other regard. "Would he really marry someone simply to build a house?"

The Prince chuckled. "No, I don't think so, but he was certainly looking for ways to recover what his family had lost."

"Apparently a Mr. Henri dealt with the conveyance. Do you know him?"

"I don't know such people," he said chidingly.

"Would Marie kill Drecsay?" she asked, but she already knew the answer. She just wanted to see what he said.

"Without Drecsay, his girlfriend loses everything. Maybe he was going to drop her."

"I haven't heard any indication from anyone I've spoken to."

The look he gave her was almost belligerent. "Well, good luck with finding some place to hide." She knew that sounded a little bit like an insult, but she didn't care. There was nothing likable about the man in her book. In saying that, she did recognize the position he was in. At least she could go home. He had no home and had to run as far as he could.

"And to you, Miss Sparks. Best of luck finding your way home. An invading army is never gentle on the women."

The warning was stark and she knew it was intended to be. She gave him a nod and kept walking, wondering if there was any way he had killed Drecsay. There was nothing to indicate a motive. The Prince was much better off financially, and it certainly didn't seem that he had any jealousy. Nothing seemed to stick there—as unpleasant a man as he was.

Lady Pettifer and Livinia hadn't even gotten inside the building by the time Dory got there.

"The Government is organizing transport," Lady Pettifer said. "They just can't give us any details yet. He knows remarkably little. I'm not sure the advent of a war had actually occurred to him."

"So what are we supposed to do? Go home and wait, they say. Unbelievable. Mrs. Grifton said she was going to drive to Calais."

"Stupid woman," Lady Pettifer said. "They are not going to let her anywhere near Calais."

"I hope you told her," Dory said.

"I doubt she listened. Some people cannot help but do the worst thing for themselves."

"Well, what are we going to do?" Livinia asked.

"I think we are better off doing as Major Dodds says. I do believe the Government is organizing something."

"If they're not too busy with other things," Livinia said pointedly, "like fighting a war."

"There are over a thousand people here. They will have to do something," Lady Pettifer said.

"So we drove all the way here for that—'return home and wait for them to do something.'" Livinia said tartly. "If they would have answered their telephone, it would have saved us a trip here."

"Not much else we can do," Lady Pettifer said with a smile. "Where are you parked?"

"Down this way," Dory said indicating, "but I can go get the car if you wish."

"No, a walk will do me good."

They set off at a leisurely pace. "Can we really afford to wait?" she asked.

"It might be better than setting off like scared rabbits, hurtling ourselves all over France. Who is to say there is any passenger transport if we even reach the northern coast, to get stuck there as the fighting begins in earnest. At least this way, the Government will send something specifically to take us home."

"I suppose you are right," Dory conceded.

The café where she had seen Prince Barenoli was now empty, which was probably a good thing, because Livinia, for some reason, seemed blind to the man's glaring faults. Dory suspected she saw the looks and the title and didn't notice the unpleasantness of the man underneath. That was the kind of man who used women like Livinia and afterward deriding them for their own gullibility and greed. Livinia utterly failed to see such things—perhaps it was her own sense of entitlement falling prey to an even larger sense of entitlement.

"I saw Prince Barenoli before," Dory said.

"Oh, he's here?" Livinia said, looking around.

"He mentioned that Drecsay intended to build on the land that the countess had bought him in Antibes, but he said it was useless land and she had bought it, a little to spite his ambition to build his own house. She bought him a few such places."

"Strange people," Lady Pettifer said with distaste.

"There is something about this that needles at me. I don't know what, but I feel it." Dory chewed her lip. There was something that wasn't clicking into place. "I must find this Mr. Henri and get a list of all his assets."

"What use to anyone is a bunch of useless land?" Livinia said. "Besides, it wasn't as though anyone would inherit. I suppose his extended family would inherit. They are the only ones who had anything to gain."

Dory drove them back along the coast, deep in thought.

Chapter 24

The consulate's telephone remained permanently engaged. It was impossible to reach them, but Lady Pettifer used her trusted network of friends to garner what information was available. The Government had committed to sending transport to Nice to pick up anyone needing to be conveyed back to the UK.

Each night, they listened diligently to the BBC, heard how the Grand Duchess Charlotte of Luxembourg and her family had fled across France as the occupation of Luxembourg had started. The resignation of Neville Chamberlain and the appointment of Winston Churchill as the new Prime Minister. Para shooting troops being defeated. Intense fighting between the Dutch and Belgium troops against the Germans. The Kaiser being offered asylum and the Norwegian and Dutch Governments shifting to London.

There was so much happening every day, they had a hard time keeping up. It seemed as though the world was devolving in front of them. They listened to the French news also, which tended to focus more on the battles in its neighboring countries and the movement of troops eastward in the country.

They sat with their sherries and listened in horror. There was nothing they could do but sit and listen, and wait for this ship that was supposed to arrive. How a ship would transport over a thousand people, Dory didn't know. They intently listened for any news about Switzerland to see whatever hell Vivian was heading toward, but Switzerland wasn't mentioned. Whatever agreement they had with the Germans was keeping them out of this war. It couldn't simply be their ferocious army that was keeping the Germans away. Or perhaps they simply didn't want to deal with the Alps.

Dory didn't dare think what would happen if the ship didn't come. Spain was probably the best answer. It seemed Franco was intent on not getting involved. Every day, more and more people chose to flee instead of wait for the ship. Lady Pettifer felt it was safer to wait, trusted the British Government's promises more than the French officials' lack of concern for the British expats.

Sleepless nights continued and Dory woke feeling exhausted and bleary-eyed in the mornings. The waiting was awful, but another day started and there was no news of a ship arriving. In fact, there was little news at all. Apparently, Major Dodds kept reassuring people that the ship was on the way, but it would take some time to get there.

Even Livinia stayed at home, although she couldn't bear to hide in her boredom. With great sighs, she wandered from room to room, wondering when Richard would come to visit. Instead of banding them all together, the occurring events were making them all seek their own solitude.

It felt wrong to do joyous things like swimming or even reading, so Dory turned her attention to Baron Drecsay and the puzzle it still posed. She wanted to write to DI Ridley about what she had learned, but she felt as though she shouldn't. He would be too distracted to worry about what she was doing. When they'd spoken, though, he'd offered to listen.

With this in mind, she grabbed the receiver and rang through to the operator. At this point, she didn't really know who she wanted to call, but she asked for the office of the prosecutor in Nice and to her surprise was put through straight away.

The woman who answered wasn't impressed when Dory asked if anyone knew of a solicitor called Mr. Henri. Grudgingly, Dory was passed to another woman, and then another, who surprisingly had heard of a Mr. Henri, who had offices in Marseille.

"Oh," Dory said. In all honesty, she hadn't expected this to work, but here she was—a step closer. Thanking the woman, Dory hung up and called the operator yet again, this time asking for Marseilles, where asking for Advokat Monsieur Henri got her put forward to his office. It was ludicrously simple once she put her mind to it and imagined who could help.

A receptionist answered, but Monsieur Henri was not available just at the time. The woman took Dory's details and promised that he would call her at the earliest opportunity.

With a nervous sigh, Dory paced. It seemed nothing she did would alleviate the pervasive nervousness in her, but she knew it had nothing to do with waiting for Mr. Henri's call—even though she did highly anticipate this upcoming conversation. There was no indication how long the man would be in returning her call. It could be he was engaging in blind panic like so many others.

Dory imagined him haphazardly packing up his office and preparing to flee. Probably not. He appeared to be French, so there was nowhere he would go. For a moment, Dory felt the gravity of the situation that was unfolding north of them. She hoped the poor Luxembourgian and the Belgian peoples were alright, able to imagine the blind panic there. Perhaps it was unkind of her to think derisively about people's unthinking need for action.

"Stop that incessant pacing," Lady Pettifer called from the salon and Dory went over to sit with her.

"Sorry," she said. "I just can't seem to relax."

"That's hardly surprising, I suppose."

The telephone rang and Dory flew up to reach it before Mr. Fernley had a chance.

"Yes," she said when the man on the other end asked for Miss Dory Sparks.

"How can I be of assistance?" he continued.

"Well, I am actually calling about Baron Drecsay. I am sure you are aware of what's happened."

"I am," the man confirmed. Dory could hear the suspicion in his voice.

Again Dory struggled for words. "I wished to ask you about the properties that he had been… given by Countess Tirau."

"Yes," the man said yet again, waiting for her to come to the point.

"Uhh, I heard there were a few properties. One in Antibes and also an island in Scotland."

"That is correct."

"And you handled the conveyance for these properties?"

"Yes." A sigh of annoyed resignation sounded through the phone.

"What other properties were there?"

"Why do you wish to know?"

"Oh, I am investigating his death on behalf of his family." The lie had become familiar now and she was essentially the self-appointed private investigator for the family.

"I see. There are also three properties in Hungary, an apartment in Paris, and a parcel of land in Palestine."

Dory's eyebrows rose. The Baron wasn't exactly destitute. "And all of these properties were gifts from the countess?"

"Yes. This does not cover the properties belonging to the title in Hungary, which are extensive."

"And all of the properties go to the next baron? I understand he had no children or family."

"I do not deal with the succession of the title and his properties, as such, but I understand his heir was a cousin. You will have to direct your queries to his solicitor in Hungary."

"So there is nothing untoward about any of these properties?"

"Not that I know of. They are all quite impractical. There were, of course, some liens from creditors, so the heir will not receive all of the properties. The baron did have debts. His finances were disorderly, frankly. I am still dealing with the liens, and more creditors are coming forward."

"It appears some of the baron's jewelry has been unaccounted for."

"Yes, that seems to be true, but that is an issue for the new baron to take up with the police."

"Can you tell me about the creditors?"

"I don't remember off the top of my head, but I will ask my assistant to send you a list of creditors and their claims."

"That would be much appreciated," Dory said with a smile. Mr. Henri had run out of patience with her, so she thanked him and let him go.

"Anything interesting?" Lady Pettifer called and Dory returned to the salon with the piece of paper on which she had scribbled everything Mr. Henri had said.

"There are a number of properties—an apartment in Paris, the property in Antibes, the Scottish Island, a number of properties in Hungary, and lastly a parcel of land in Palestine."

"Palestine? Why in God's name would he have land in Palestine?"

"Well, the countess seemed to like to give him properties he could not use."

"So you think one of these properties is the reason he was killed?"

With a sigh, Dory sat down heavily. "I don't know. I can't find any other reason. His relationships seemed quite stable. He was interested in Livinia, and we didn't kill him. Unless there is someone jealous of that."

"Like Richard?"

They both chuckled.

"Well, Richard really didn't like Drecsay, but I can't imagine him killing for it," Dory said. "But then he was there. He had opportunity."

"Livinia and Drecsay had only gotten to know each other. It is difficult to imagine that Richard was so incensed he would destroy his rival."

"It hadn't even occurred to me to think of Richard as a suspect, but I suppose I must. He had opportunity," Dory said. "And a semblance of a motive."

"It would be an unhinged mind who would murder for such a reason."

Could it be that Richard was hiding such a dark urge behind a good-natured façade? It was something that had to be considered.

Chapter 25

The detailed list of the properties arrived from Mr. Henri a few days later. Included was a list of creditor liens against Baron Drecsay. They arrived in a large manila envelope that Mr. Fernley delivered with the rest of the post. The postal service hadn't ceased. Normalcy was highly appreciated, seen as a sign that the world wasn't entirely falling apart.

Dory and Lady Pettifer sat in the covered area outside, the shade and the breeze keeping them cool. Midday was starting to be a period for staying in the shade. Livinia's music played above their heads. Like this, everything seemed perfectly normal. It was almost a cruel illusion.

"So what have we?" Lady Pettifer asked as Dory unwound the tie of the envelope and pulled out the sheets of paper inside.

"Here are the properties. The property in Antibes. Five acres some seven miles away from the coast. It is currently an overgrown orchard. It has access to Chermin des Combes."

"Not particularly valuable," Lady Pettifer said.

"The apartment in Paris. Place Vendôme."

"Well, that is nothing to scoff at. It must be worth quite a bit."

"Two rooms."

"Just a bolt hole, then."

"In Hungary, a farm. No, two farms. Quite sizeable."

"I don't think the properties in Hungary will be of any interest to anyone here," Lady Pettifer stated.

"The land in Palestine, which is down to the south, one hundred and fifty miles from the Egyptian border."

"That's nothing but desert. It's not even close to any significant town as far as I know. How much land?

"Twenty-two acres," Dory read.

"Twenty-two acres of desert. I'm surprised she didn't buy him half the Sahara. Is that it?"

"There is the island in Scotland. Unnamed Island, it says. And then it gives coordinates."

"I'm assuming no one is fighting over that one if no one can bother naming it. And the liens."

Dory found the other sheet of paper.

"Well, the Hotel Contano has put a claim in to the estate, but not to a specific piece of property. A number of retailers in Nice have done the same. Prince Barenoli has a lien against the Parisian apartment," Dory said with surprise. "He mentioned nothing about that. If fact, didn't he say something about anyone giving Drecsay money being stupid? Didn't mention he was referring to himself."

"The Prince has money, but some people are averse to losing it."

For a moment, Dory considered what Lady Pettifer said, trying to see if she could find a motive there. "The apartment is worth something, but not a great deal."

"An apartment like that is not something he would choose to stay in. His intention would be to sell it and realize the money."

"He hadn't mentioned any of this."

"I'm sure he dismisses it as nothing, but he must be aware that it does give him some degree of motive."

Hardly convincing, Dory thought. Nothing they had found so far was directly suggested a motive for murder. "Then the land in Palestine. Oh," Dory said as she saw the name. "Terry Wilcott has placed a lien against it. Also something he didn't mention when I spoke to him."

"Why specifically that?" Lady Pettifer asked.

With a gust of wind, Livinia arrived from inside the house. "What are you talking about?" she said as she sat down.

"Terry Wilcott had taken a lien out against one of Baron Drecsay's properties," Dory said.

The scones were more interesting to Livinia than any lien Terry had placed. "Seems everyone is circling like vultures now that he's dead."

"Well, the Prince is as well," Dory stated.

"Is he? Drecsay must have owed him money."

"It seems Drecsay owed quite a few people money."

Livinia was conspicuously quiet on this subject. To her, it didn't really matter now, Dory supposed. Money wasn't something she readily thought about. It simply appeared when she needed it.

"I think I would like to speak to Terry again," Dory said, turning her attention to Lady Pettifer to see if she agreed with her assessment of the next step.

"I suppose I can take you to see him. He has a house in Cannes." Livinia said.

In a sense, Dory was glad she didn't have to go all the way to Nice. Cannes was much closer and it wouldn't take them long to go there and back. Nice required more planning.

"Actually, it would be nice to get out of the house for a bit. We've been cooped up here for days on end."

"Why don't you set off now," Lady Pettifer suggested. "I might go upstairs and rest."

"Marvellous," Livinia sang and rose with her half-eaten scone still in her hand. "Come on, Dory. I'll drive." Livinia was already marching through the house to the other side.

With a wince, Dory grabbed her hat and followed. She hated it when Livinia drove, but Terry was Livinia's friend and Dory wasn't entirely sure how he would behave if it was just her alone.

They drove down the coast and it was lovely. The sun shone, the breeze was cooling. The water glittered where the sun reflected.

"I was going spare in the house all day long," Livinia said, clearly joyful about getting out. "No one is doing anything at the moment. Everything feels so suppressed. I hope this war doesn't go on forever."

In fact, there were troops in Cannes. Dory hadn't seen this before. Endless men dressed in olive green uniforms, with trucks the same color. They had helmets and weapons.

"What are they doing down here?" Livinia uttered.

"I think they must be guarding against the Italians," Dory said quietly. It was disconcerting seeing them. The war was encroaching on the coast as well. They had to be quite worried about the Italians to send so many troops. They passed endless rows of parked trucks with green canvas canopies.

With a sharp turn, Livinia drove down a street leading away from the promenade, until she stopped in front of a white house. It was modest in comparison to Archie Wilshire's house. Nice, in quite a modern style with large windows in what had to be the salon.

With light steps, Livinia walked up the marble stairs to the front door and worked the iron knocker. A butler appeared and Livinia stated their business.

They were led through to the salon with the large windows, which was a lovely room with wood paneling and endless carpets. Terry had good taste in furniture. Everything looked modern and clean.

"Livinia," he said as he rose from his sofa where he was reading the local paper. "And you brought the charming Miss Sparks." His tone defied his statement. He didn't think her charming at all. In fact, he didn't quite know why she was there.

"Dory had a few questions she wanted to put to you."

"Oh?" he said with raised eyebrows. "Regarding?"

"The lien you placed against Baron Drecsay's property," Dory said.

"Oh that," Terry said and visibly relaxed back into the sofa. "What can I tell you? He owed me some money."

"Why the land in Palestine?"

"Uhh," he said in a drawn-out manner. "Well, he didn't owe me a great deal. Two hundred pounds and it seemed to be the property that best approximated the sum."

"You didn't see fit to forgive the sum?" Dory wasn't sure why she asked that; she just did. Maybe because she believed Archie Wilshire would forgive such a sum to a friend, but Terry had not.

"Forgive? We never forgive a sum. Practically a family motto."

"What in the world are you going to do with a plot in Palestine?" Livinia asked.

"It's not worth a great deal. About two hundred pounds, I would assume. Unfortunately, with everything going on, I can't sell it. So I'm stuck with it for a while—at least until the war is over. Drinks, anyone?"

"Yes, a martini would be marvelous," Livinia said.

"Maybe just a splash of gin in some tonic," Dory said, knowing she would be driving home, and Livinia would not be wanting to return to the house in the next two hours.

Terry and Livinia started talking about their friends and what everyone was doing. Archie Wilshire had gone, and taken his wife with him. He was a pilot as it turned out and simply flew his own plane north. Dory hoped it was safe to fly planes across the country now. It was a question that had to be asked of even the mundane things. Surely no one would fire at a small aircraft flying north, but you couldn't take these things for granted.

Like them, Terry was going to wait for the ship to come, which in intervening days had turned into two ships that were definitely being diverted to the coast to pick them up. Everyone sounded so sure. The consulate had even called the house to assure them that the ships were coming and they all had to—absolutely had to—leave on the ships, or they would themselves be responsible for any consequences for staying put.

Means of leaving would be limited after the ships sailed, the consulate had said. Lady Pettifer had learned that some of the older residents were staying put anyway. Many had nothing to return to and would be destitute in England without income or shelter. Taking the risk of staying was simply the easiest option. Dory felt inordinately sorry for them, knowing they had to face down whatever storm came this way.

How bad could it be, some asked. Except there had been worrying reports about the Germans actually attacking civilians in some town up north. It was perhaps the most shocking thing Dory had ever heard and Lady Pettifer had grown increasingly dismayed. That was not within the rules of warfare, but the Germans seemed to have little regard for honor in war. Staying put with such a force coming, might be a disastrous decision. Still, they refused to change their minds.

Chapter 26

The story around Baron Drecsay was like an onion, uncovering new layers the deeper she dug, but the layers never seemed to present themselves fully. There were a number of people who were financially better off with the baron dead, but none of the sums involved were big enough to justify murder, and none of the players appeared disturbed enough to kill someone for such a paltry sum.

"Nothing stands out particularly," Lady Pettifer said as Dory wrote out all the things they had learned. "Even Marie Chard, if she was the one who stole the jewelry. It could be that she robbed the baron while he was at the masquerade. But then she couldn't have snuck into the party unseen and killed him. Lady Tonbridge's butler would never let a girl like that in if she simply appeared at the door without an invitation. Let's face it: she's a girl with a certain reputation and Lady Tonbridge would never abide having such a girl at her party."

"All our other suspects were at the party, but none seem to have a credible reason for killing him."

"I have a feeling we will never know who the killer is until we establish proper motive."

"Maybe I need to talk to Marie again," Dory said with a sigh. "She knew him best. I didn't ask her about any of the properties other than the land in Antibes."

"I suppose we could try to see if anyone has sold the baron's jewelry," Lady Pettifer said, reaching for a biscuit from the tea tray.

"I don't mind telling you it's getting quite frightening driving through Cannes now. The place is full of soldiers. There's probably more in Nice."

"No doubt. Perhaps we should think of them as being here to protect us."

Dory wasn't entirely convinced by the assertion.

"I have to admit," Lady Pettifer stated. "It is the perfect time to commit a murder. No one has the time to look into it."

"Except for us. Poor Baron Drecsay ended up with inept investigators," Dory lamented.

"Don't sell yourself short. You are doing more for this man than anyone—probably more than he deserved, to be completely honest."

"You don't mean that," Dory said.

"No, I suppose not. We must persevere. You should go speak to the girl. Take Livinia with you."

With a smile, Dory wondered if Lady Pettifer was so keen for her to speak to Marie simply to get rid of Livinia for a while. Livinia's boredom was trying for all of them.

After finishing her tea, Dory rose and went upstairs in search for Livinia.

*

Again, Livinia drove and Dory sat with her hand clenched over the top of her door. At least Dory ended up driving home whenever they went on one of their outings.

Alcohol invariably appeared somewhere and Livinia was quite happy to hand over for the return journey.

Charlotte Ginsborough was the person Livinia was determined to see. Dory vaguely knew the girl, but had never had much to do with her.

This time, there appeared to be more people in Nice—simply walking or standing around in groups. The crowd in front of the consulate was even larger, and some had their bags with them. Surely the ship wasn't coming right now.

"They're not British," Livinia said as they slowly drove past.

A frown marred Dory's face. Why were they there, she wondered. They were seeking visas to go to Britain. "Do you think they're Belgians?"

"I think they might be Jews," Livinia said. "They're not waiting around to find out what the Germans will do to them. Poor sods. They've had to leave everything and run."

Dory craned her neck to watch as they drove past. "There's so many. Do you think the ships coming will take them all?"

"I guess that depends on how large the ships are."

Now she watched all the people on the street and many of them looked foreign. Their dress wasn't right for the climate, and they tended to wear what looked like their sturdiest clothes, and there were children—lots and lots of children.

"Where shall I drop you?" Livinia asked.

"I can hop out here and take the tram to Riquiers," Dory said and Livinia pulled over. They agreed to meet again in two hours.

The tram was also full of people, strangers who were consulting maps. They had all their suitcases with them. Dory expected they had all come down on the train. The BBC had mentioned bombings in Rotterdam and Dory expected all these people fled from there. It wouldn't just be Jewish people—everyone needed to escape the Germans. Each night the news got worse and worse. Insanity seemed to be progressing relentlessly, and here were the people escaping it. It was the first true sign that everything they heard on the wireless was true. The people running away from the madness were sitting all around her.

Getting off at Riquier, she made her way to Marie's house and knocked. No one answered. They weren't home or weren't answering. She stated it was her, but still no one came to the door. Had they left?

Dory spent an hour sitting in the doorway to see if either Marie or her mother returned, but they didn't come. Eventually Dory had to give up. This trip had been a dud, a waste of time, so she returned to the spot where Livinia was supposed to pick her up and waited yet again. Sitting down, she watched people. Well, all those empty hotel rooms that the visitors to the coast had deserted in the autumn would be filling up again, but these people weren't here for a pleasant time, they were running for their lives. This all sat very heavily. Some would secure visas and leave, others would have to stay. The Germans were still very far away, so people were safer down here than in their homes. Hopefully it would stay that way.

Livinia finally arrived and was perfectly intent on driving back as well. "People are pouring out of every train that arrives," she said. "It must be an uncomfortable journey all crammed in like sardines. What did you learn from Marie?"

"Nothing. She wasn't there."

"Maybe she left. The Belgians are all trying to come here and we're all trying to leave."

"All these people," Dory said. "Where are they all going to go?"

"Maybe they have family in Britain."

"Maybe. Although if your town is being bombed, I think you'd go even if you didn't."

"Charlotte is waiting for the ships, too. She still thinks Drecsay was a spy, but she couldn't really say why." They had clearly been talking about it. "She did mention something funny, though."

"What?"

"When I mentioned Palestine, she recalled some cartographer that Drecsay had made an acquaintance with some while back. Last year, she said. Anyway, this man had just come from Palestine."

"A cartographer?"

"Something such. Charlotte wasn't entirely sure, but she said he was the type of man who thought well of himself and always wore jodhpurs. Adventurer type."

"Did she catch a name?"

"No. She just mentioned she'd seen them speaking in cafes a few times. Drecsay liked to frequent a café that was close to her apartments. Not that they really knew each other. She said Drecsay was always very polite and friendly."

To an heiress like Charlotte? How was that not a surprise.

A cartographer, Dory thought, trying to turn this over in her head. Why would Drecsay make the acquaintance of a cartographer who'd just come from Palestine? The question kept presenting itself over and over again, but no answers appeared.

The sun was still warm as they returned and Lady Pettifer was sitting on the covered patio with her tea.

"All of Nice is full of Jews," Livinia said when they arrived. "They're coming down on the trains."

"Poor things," Lady Pettifer said. "I suppose they will now face the same persecution as those in Germany, stripped of their jobs, wealth and property."

"The stories from Poland say they can fare worse," Dory said with a shudder. Magazine articles she'd read mentioned horrific things that the Germans did in Poland. People were right to flee.

"So what did you learn?" Lady Pettifer asked.

"Well, Marie was not at home, but Livinia's friend mentioned Drecsay befriending some adventurer type who had just returned from Palestine."

"A cartographer," Livinia added.

"A cartographer?" Lady Pettifer said with surprise.

"I'll just get Mr. Henri's notes," Dory said and went to retrieve them from the desk in the study. Returning, she sat down and turned to the sheet mentioning the property in Palestine. "Oh," she said. "It appears the property was bought last year. In the autumn. So a random property in Palestine was bought just as he made the acquaintance of some adventurer type coming from there. That seems too much of a coincidence. They have to be linked."

"Unless Countess Tirau noted the relationship and bought him a property on a whim," Lady Pettifer. "She seemed to be of that unique disposition."

"I'll call Mr. Henri to see if he knows something about how the property came about." Rising again, she walked over to the phone and asked for the operator in Marseille so she could be put through to his office.

"What do you want, Miss Sparks?" he said with annoyance when his secretary put her through. Dory hadn't expected the tone.

"I am sorry if I am bothering you, I just wanted some more information about Baron Drecsay's property in Palestine."

With a sigh, she heard him sit down. "Umm," he said after a while as if trying to recall something from a very long time ago. "Yes, the property. They bought it not so long ago."

"Was it the countess' idea to buy it and how did she find it?"

"I think this one was actually Drecsay's idea. He was very specific about the land he wanted, had coordinates."

"Coordinates? So the countess bought it at his request?"

"I believe so. I cannot be assured. But as opposed to the other properties, Drecsay came to see me personally to make sure everything was in order. Now, I'm sorry, I can't help you more. I have a hundred things to do. It seems the whole country wants to request exit visas."

"Oh, of course. I won't take more of your time." After a quick goodbye, she hung up. All those people who had come off the trains were seeking the help of solicitors to secure exit visas. The man had to be run off his feet. She fully understood how annoying she would be at such a time. If she had the chance, she would send him a bottle of wine for the trouble.

Dory returned to the patio. "Mr. Henri recalls that Baron Drecsay initiated this purchase."

"So it was different from the other properties," Lady Pettifer said. "It is still land in the middle of nowhere. Useless for all intents and purposes. What would a cartographer want with such land?"

"Well, we don't know why he wanted it," Dory said, pointing out the assumption, "but it seemed Drecsay bought this land based on his conversations with the cartographer."

"If we just knew his name," Lady Pettifer said.

"The High Commission in Palestine might know if any cartographers were surveying in the district," Livinia pointed out.

Chapter 27

The Germans were bombing in England. The news was horrific and depressing that night. Dory wasn't sure she had heard something this distressing since the war was declared. The British forces were in retreat, withdrawing to Dunkirk, the Germans hitting them with a constant bombardment. There was also a report stating that the Germans were massacring the inhabitants of a Belgian village called Vinkt. This was stated by the French radio. The BBC was curiously silent on the topic, which made Dory wonder what else they weren't being told if it didn't bear mentioning when innocent villagers were rounded up and massacred.

The next day, Belgium surrendered with King Leopold being taken and interred by the Nazis.

Each newspaper and radio news program were started with even more dread. The news only got worse and worse. The British were evacuating from the continent. There was too much bad news, and at the same time not enough news. They went for hours without hearing a thing, knowing something catastrophic could have happened.

All along, the sunshine and serenity of Villa Bellevieu were as it always was. They had no visitors, nor did they go anywhere. It was almost as if they lived in a perfect, little bubble, interspersed by horridness coming through the wireless or papers.

There was an unusual amount of cars driving along the coast road. They could see it from a specific spot in the garden, and it looked like quite a few military trucks. The whole country was on the move. The French had to be worried about the Italians, who so far seemed to want to stay out of this war, but Navy ships patrolled out at sea.

A man named Bovis called from the consulate to inform them that the evacuation ships were on their way and would be there in about ten days. He stressed how they had to be there and that there would be no help from the Government from then on if they missed the ship. Dory assured him that they would be there.

They could do nothing but wait. The international telephone lines were increasingly hard to book and mail stopped arriving. Dory tried to turn her attention to Drecsay, but there was too much worry. She had no luck trying to get hold of the High Commission in Palestine, and the mailman refused to take the letter she'd written, saying he could only deliver within the Vichy Government territory.

"Perhaps if we cannot send letters, we could still use telegrams," Lady Pettifer said. "We could send one to the High Commission in Palestine to see if they know this man, or if they are aware of anything noteworthy about this property that Baron Drecsay bought."

Dory nodded. "Then again, what could a cartographer tell Drecsay that would make him rush out and purchase the property?"

"Well, Terry Wilcott had a lien on the property, so it's now technically his. Perhaps we need to mention this in the telegram."

"It's going to be expensive," Dory said, trying to think of ways to say all that in as few words as possible."

"Now is not the time for frugality," Lady Pettifer said and rose. "We are running out of time. The ship is here in mere days. Hopefully we will hear back.

"I'll drive into Cannes to the telegraph office and see if they can send it."

There was no point waiting, so Dory got in the car and took the coast road east. As before, there was an increased level of traffic. The French Navy had their port in Toulon, so it could be that many of them were going there. What did that mean? Were they preparing for something? By the look of it, they were. The most awful thing about this was that they knew so little. It was hard to decide what to do. The Germans were now bombing England and they had to wonder if they were safer where they were. The consulate seemed to think not.

Their neighbor, Mr. Merton, had decided to stay put. The idea made Lady Pettifer uneasy, but he was a grown man—an elderly man—so he did have the right to decide for himself.

These were such grave decisions and they could have catastrophic consequences if they proved wrong, especially if the most disturbing accounts of the German Army's behavior were true.

The drive to Cannes wasn't so long. Cannes was not as busy as Nice, but there were still people who didn't normally dwell there. Rooms were sought everywhere, she supposed, and there were plenty of rooms in Cannes. The cafes were also more busy than they had been a few days ago.

The telegram office was in a brick building down one of the side streets. Dory parked along the main promenade and walked. The streets could be troublesome and it wasn't worth trying to get into the township itself sometimes. Especially now that there were motorcars like black beetles parked everywhere, filled with family possessions—even mattresses strapped to roofs.

The houses were not quite as grand on the side streets. But the town looked busy, as if it had to some degree recovered from the shock of what was happening.

A piece of paper plastered on the wall of one of the building caught her attention and she passed it without really absorbing what it said in stark, black print. 'Mort aux Juifs.' Dory froze and stared at it, not believing what it said. Death to Jews. With a gasp, her fingers pressed to her mouth. This couldn't be real? Could there be someone this callous in their midst—down here where things were sane?

This piece of paper showed that there were. Around here was a person, or people, who wished ill on people they had never met, didn't know—or worse, someone they did—a neighbor. How could this be? It was so unfathomable, she had always assumed that everyone else thought it was utter madness too, but the insidious hatred was rearing its ugly head here, too.

Reaching out, she tore the paper down, unsure if she felt embarrassed as well as mortified. All those people who had come here to find sanctuary were meeting with the same hatred they had fled. It was beyond disappointing for find something like this. Instantly, suspicion formed about every person on the street. Had they put it up? Had they seen it and quietly agreed? Why hadn't they torn it down?

Feeling completely stunned, Dory kept walking to the telegraph office. It was just ahead of her and she had to focus. The shock of seeing a visual display of the hatred she couldn't understand still clouded her mind.

The place was full of people waiting, some in line, others apparently to receive something. This was going to take a while.

A number of different languages were spoken—from German, to French, and other languages she couldn't identify. Everyone was calmly waiting, slowly moving toward the desk.

"Can I help you?" A woman said behind the desk when it was Dory's turn. They were all women, Dory noticed. That was a change from the last time she'd been here—which admittedly was some time ago.

"I need to send a telegram?"

"Where to?"

Dory had trouble getting her mind working. "Uhmm, the British High Commission in Palestine."

"That is a more unusual request," the girl said and pulled out a printed form. "Write here and bring it back," she said and dismissed Dory to serve the person behind her.

"Right," Dory said and moved along. For a moment she felt silly. Here she was, trying to gain information about a piece of land when these people were obviously planning their flight to safety. How could she invest so much time in the death of one aristocrat when there was so much need for attention elsewhere? In a way, it felt wrong, but she also knew that the murderer was probably happy about the distraction the war caused. The idea that someone was benefitting from this war felt even more wrong.

Taking a moment, she devised the telegram as concisely as she could, asking if the Commission knew of a cartographer working in the area, and if there was anything of note about the land that Baron Drecsay had purchased.

It could be that they paid little attention to her request. Should she state that the baron had possibly been murdered because of this land? Then it occurred to her that it was unlikely that she and Lady Pettifer would be here by the time they replied—if they replied.

Please respond to DI Ridley at Pirbright Camp. The 'please' would cost extra, but she just couldn't bring herself to not write it. There was no one else to send it to. Vivian was God-knew-where. She, Lady Pettifer and Livinia would be on a ship for the better part of a month. She would have to use Ridley as a gathering point for any information at this point. She asked for a second telegram form and sent one to him too, saying that she was just about to board the ship to England.

Palestinian property purchased by baron after meeting cartographer returning from region, she wrote. High Commission to send details to you while at sea. Regards, Dory.

Hopefully he would figure out what that meant.

Chapter 28

And then the ships came. They could see them from the house. Two massive merchant ships, slowly sailing towards Nice.

"We best be going," Livinia said, sticking her head out the window above them. "Is everything in the car?"

"It might be best not to take so much with you," Lady Pettifer said.

"Who knows when we'll ever get to see it again?" Livinia said as if Lady Pettifer had suggested something ridiculous.

"You might not be able to find someone to carry the trunk, my dear." With a snort, Lady Pettifer turned her attention back to Dory. "And here we are screaming like fishwives."

Dory had already placed her small suitcase in the back of the car. There were some things she was leaving behind. A pair of shoes and some clothes—especially the party clothes. What use would she have of those in London when war was raging all around them? Dory still didn't know if they were heading toward a more dangerous situation than they were leaving, but it felt important to be at home and not stuck on foreign soil.

"Best go see to Mr. Merton," Lady Pettifer suggested. "Try to see if you can convince him to come with us."

With a nod, Dory rose and hurriedly walked over to the path that led to Mr. Merton's property. It would take a few minutes to get there, but eventually she reached the stone two-story house. It was nowhere near as grand as Lady Pettifer's villa, but the old man seemed happy enough here.

A knock on the door was met with silence. "Mr. Merton?" Again there was silence. Had he gone to meet the ship on his own? He had been so adamant he wasn't going to go.

"Mr. Merton?" she called as she walked around the house, finding Mr. Merton standing in his chicken coup with his trousers rolled up and wearing wellingtons. "There you are?"

"Miss Sparks," he grumbled. He had never been remotely pleasant, but Dory had grown to expect that.

"We are about to leave for the ship. Are you sure you won't come with us?"

"Some bunch of Jerrys aren't going to chase me off my land," he stated pompously. "Never."

"Major Dodds recommends that everyone leaves. You can come back when things are settled again."

"What's he going to do? Come down here and drag me away?"

"No, of course not. He's only thinking with your best interest at heart."

The man grumbled again. "Well, you can tell him where he can stick it."

"I take it that's a no, then."

"Damned right."

Dory sighed. Nothing was going to convince the man, but was he the one making the wiser choice? "If you run out of supplies, Lady Pettifer's stores are still well stocked."

"I'm sure I'll be fine. My chickens won't stop laying because the Jerrys are making a hoo hah."

"I hope so," Dory said absently. "If you're sure?"

"Off you go. Run like scared little rabbits."

"Alright, then. If you insist."

He turned his back on her and Dory made her way back to the path. That was a waste of time even before she started, but she supposed they had to try.

Livinia was downstairs by the time Dory got back, dressed in a summery dress with yellow lemons printed on the material. She looked impossibly smart. "You'll help carry my trunk, won't you, Dory? If it comes to it."

"Sure," Dory said.

"See," Livinia said as if turning to Lady Pettifer in victory.

"We had better get going if we are going to beat the ships to Nice," Lady Pettifer said. "Mr. Fernley? Are you ready?"

"Just about, madame," he called from inside. He had spent the morning placing sheets over the furniture along with Babette from the village. Babette would essentially be the caretaker while they were gone. She normally served that role when Lady Pettifer left for England, but it would be longer than just over the summer this time.

Babette appeared carrying Beauty in a cage and placed it in the back.. "The house will be dusted every week," she said with assurance.

"I know I can trust you, Babette. Take all the perishables when you leave. I don't know how much we have. And if you should ever need to, you can take from the stores as required."

"Thank you, Madame," she said with a quick nod. "I will lock up when you go."

They walked through to the hallway, where Lady Pettifer grabbed her handbag and umbrella. It looked out of place in this weather, but you always needed an umbrella where they were going. "Goodbye, house. I shall miss you. Hopefully it won't be too long before we're reunited."

Guiseppe from the village was there, too. He was to drive them and then return the motorcar to the house. "And we go," he said, holding his brown cigarette between his fingers as he drove. A veteran of the Great War, he drove better than Livinia did, even as he didn't have ready access to a car otherwise.

The acrid smoke from the cigarette wafted back to them occasionally, but telling a French man not to smoke was a waste of breath. Mr. Fernley sat in the small folded up seat at the very back of the car with Beauty. It was unusual to have the butler and the dog with them on an outing, but this wasn't just some outing—they were all fleeing France just like everyone else.

"I wonder if we will see Lady Summernot after all, or if she managed to secure passage prior. I hope Clara Winch manages to make it down. She is so old. Mr. Fernley, perhaps we should go past her apartments to see if she needs assistance. Her knees are dreadful."

"Of course," Mr. Fernley said behind them.

There was a nervous tension in the car. No one spoke and Guiseppe threw his cigarette over the side of the door and lit another.

*

The port was on the other side of Nice, and there were abandoned cars as they drove closer. Quite a few people were leaving everything behind without an expectation that they were coming back. Guiseppe was made to detour down a road where Mrs. Winch lived, and Mr. Fernley climbed out and rang her bell. No one answered.

"That puts my mind to rest," Lady Pettifer said. "Perhaps she took a taxi."

"They are having a busy day, I expect," Livinia said.

Driving on, they reached the port and it was inordinately busy. A crowd was waiting and a man stood with a clipboard, searching for names. Dory recognized him from the consulate. As British citizens, they didn't need the exit visas that the French or Belgians sought. Technically, they weren't emigrating.

French policemen were standing nearby, watching the people swarm around the gateway manned by the consulate man. Everyone was trying to get his attention, to speak to him, some with money in their hands. There were people here without visas, Dory realized. Desperate to get away, they tried to plead.

Spotting them, the consulate man waved them forward. Somehow, Mr. Fernley and Dory had ended up carrying Livinia's trunk, while also carrying their own luggage, and Beauty's cage on top. To Livinia's consternation, she ended up carrying Lady Pettifer's luggage.

They had to jostle through the crowd to the front where they presented their passports. The man carefully checked each one and ticked off their names on the clipboard before giving Lady Pettifer a note and telling her to give it to the man at the top of the gangway. "Go through," he said.

They walked through to join an even larger crowd. There had to be at least a thousand people there—more even. A ship was berthed next to the port and a string of people were walking up the gangplank.

It was not a passenger ship. There would be no comfortable cabins for them to retreat to like they had had on the voyage over two years back. This was a standard cargo ship—and they were the cargo.

With a sigh, Dory surveyed the scene. It was going to be an extremely uncomfortable voyage back to the UK. Mr. Fernley went to register Beauty with the ship's crew. Luckily, Lady Pettifer had had the foresight to sort the dog's papers as soon as the war had initially been declared. Taking her would mean a month's quarantine when they arrived in Britain, but who knew how long this war would last, Lady Pettifer had said when they'd talked about what to do with Beauty. If it really would take years, Lady Pettifer didn't want to be without the comfort of her dog.

It took a good hour to reach the gangplank and they had to awkwardly scramble up while carrying Livinia's trunk. Dory's heels were skidding slightly until they found grip. It was an uncomfortable assent, and Lady Pettifer was exhausted by the time they made it onboard.

The ship was entirely functional. As expected, there were no passenger cabins. Most had to find their places crammed together in large storerooms where they had to find space where they could. This was what the Government could spare at the moment—a ship at its barest minimum. Lady Pettifer was led to a small room with two births on top of each other and a small porthole. There was barely enough room to walk and the three of them together filled the whole cabin.

"Your trunk will have to be outside," Lady Pettifer said.

"Everyone will rifle through it," Livinia whined. "I'll be surprised if I have anything left by the time we reach England. This is horrific. There are three of us and two beds."

"I can sleep on the floor, I suppose," Dory said. "With some blankets, I'm sure it will be comfortable."

"Perhaps we can form a mattress with some of your clothes," Lady Pettifer suggested to Livinia. "Then they will be inside the cabin after all."

Livinia wasn't pleased with the suggestion, which wasn't surprising considering how dusty the floor was. The porthole didn't open, so there was no way of clearing the mustiness. They must be occupying the sleeping quarters of some burly and sweaty sailors.

Looking around, Lady Pettifer sighed. There was nowhere for them to sit other than on the lower bunk. "I have never before been subject to the Government's hospitality. Admittedly, it is grim, but we must be grateful that they are evacuating us, and that they have given us one of the cabins. Not everyone is given that consideration."

Chapter 29

They were served soup with rolls the next day after what could only be described as an uncomfortable sleep. Lady Pettifer snored at close quarters, it turned out. The cabin also remained disturbingly warm during the night, made worse as the Mediterranean sun rose in the morning.

As soon as they woke, they opened the cabin door to try to get some air in. It did help even if there were the occasional wafts of marine diesel. The smell of the sea was lovely. The Mediterranean was a deep blue color and the water rushed against the hull of the ship when Dory looked down over the railing.

All of the external walkways were crowded with people seeking respite from the dark and dingy storage rooms. Some even chose to sit down along the walls and spend the whole day there, slowly watching the coastline move past. The second ship wasn't far behind them, looking like a great leviathan swimming along the water. It wasn't a particularly beautiful ship.

Three weeks on board this ship was going to be trying, probably more so because Livinia was distinctly unhappy with the setup. Luckily, she found an acquaintance in another part of the ship, so she spent periods of time away from them.

Because it was hard for Lady Pettifer to stand for longer periods, she stayed in their small cabin more often than not. There were no seating areas. Every available space was now someone's sleeping area, including the galley.

It really was a far cry from the comforts of the trip to Nice, but at least they were on their way home. Dory knew in her heart that she wouldn't be returning to Nice. It was time to go home, and she'd known that for quite a while. What she would do when she got there, she still didn't know. Need had outpaced her planning.

Returning to the cabin, Dory found that Livinia was back. "And I saw Mrs. Vismouth. You must go say hello to her at some point. I can show you where she is."

"Perhaps later," Lady Pettifer replied. "I wish I had brought more books."

"Maybe we can create a library. I am sure hordes of people have brought books that they will finish. We can all swap," Livinia carried on. Dory knew that Livinia was trying to cheer up Lady Pettifer and it was sweet that she was trying. She had the capacity to be sweet and considerate at times.

"I think that is an excellent idea. I would actually suggest that you organize it."

"I suppose I could. Perhaps we can find a bookshelf somewhere that can be used for the purpose. At least that would give me something to do. I am bored out of my mind already."

"It's only the first day," Lady Pettifer said. "I for one am still trying to think what a cartographer could have said to sway Drecsay to purchase property in Palestine. Maybe he knew something that wasn't general knowledge—such as an upcoming change in borders. There had to be a financial gain Baron Drecsay was hoping to realize. He had clearly stated that he had found some way of recuperating some of the family wealth. I just can't see what a cartographer could have imparted."

"Well, Charlotte said it was a cartographer or something such," Livinia pointed out and Lady Pettifer turned to her.

"I thought you said it was a cartographer," Dory said.

"That's what Charlotte said, but she'd really not the brightest. She couldn't exactly remember what he was, but thought it was a cartographer or something like.

Dory's eyes sought Lady Pettifer and they both knew this changed things significantly. "He could have been anything," Dory said.

"Not just anyone would be out surveying in the deserts of Palestine. Maybe even someone acting on behalf of an organization who is interested. Which meant the land would be of interest to someone, and Drecsay decided to get it before they did," Lady Pettifer said. "Or the man was a prospector."

A piece clicked into place and things made sense. The man was a prospector seeking something. Oil, gold, something. Absently, Dory's fingers stroked across her lips as thoughts churned around her head. "And Terry Wilcott placed a lien against the property."

"That could simply be a coincidence," Livinia stated. "Terry wouldn't hurt anyone. He's always had bad luck. Only he would accidentally involve himself in a murder. He's on the ship, by the way."

"He's here?" Lady Pettifer asked and Livinia nodded.

"I think he was a bit miffed that Archie Wilshire didn't give him a lift on his plane, but apparently there were weight restrictions and Terry couldn't go."

"That is unlucky," Dory said without fully meaning it.

"Now, you better go see about that bookcase, Livinia," Lady Pettifer said. "I think I would like a new book to read."

"Alright," Livinia said and left.

"It is sufficient motive for murder," Lady Pettifer said.

"The word of some fly-by-night prospector?"

"People have killed for less."

They sat in silence for a while. "We don't have any proof that Dreesay told Terry about his plans," Dory pointed out.

"I don't believe in coincidences."

"Nor do I," Dory agreed. "How do we proceed?"

"We don't have access to anything here," Lady Pettifer said. "We are entirely cut off from everything while we're at sea."

"Maybe Livinia's friend can tell us more about what she observed and heard. Perhaps Terry was there at the time."

"Terry Wilcott is onboard this ship. We must be aware of that. If he is the murderer, then he might object to us asking questions about it," Lady Pettifer said.

"Then we must be discreet. I think I should go speak to Charlotte."

There wasn't time to speak to her. They were pulling into the port of Marseille, and even from a distance, Dory could see that the entire port was full of people. Thousands. It was the most disturbing sight she had ever seen. Clearly, people were desperate to leave.

Down the walkway along the ship, she saw one of the first officers.

"Excuse me," she called to the harried looking man.

"One moment, Miss," he said as he continued what he was doing. Dory hadn't realized she had disturbed him working, but he was supervising the men throwing massive ropes down to the dock as the ship was being tied up. "How can I help you?" he said when the men below them completed their work.

"I need to send a telegram. It's important."

"You will have to brave the crowd to get to the telegram office. It's right over there," he said, pointing. "Like this, it would be a dangerous crossing. Perhaps if you had a few shillings to spare, you could send one of the ship's boys. They are nimble and quick around the docks."

"Yes, I might do that," she said and the man departed with a nod. The boys were easy to spot. They wore uniforms with sailor's hats. "Young man," she called and pulled out two pound notes from her bag and showed them to him. "I need someone to go send a telegram and they can keep the change," which would probably surmount to a whole pound. "Interested?"

"Yes, madame," he said, his eyes on the notes.

"Excellent. Now, the message." Pulling out a small notebook and pencil, she scribbled DI Ridley as recipient at Pirbright Camp, Surrey.

Not cartographer, probably prospector. Terry Wilcott likely suspect.

Dory had no idea if DI Ridley had the time to look at this, or was even in a position to receive the telegram, but she felt it was a good idea that someone knew of what they had learnt. Who knew what could happen? They were, after all, heading into waters where U-boats sunk merchant ships on a regular basis. So far, at least, they were in what should be safe waters, but as they neared the Channel, things could get dicey. It was too scary to think about.

If nothing else, DI Ridley could follow up and then report to the extended Drecsay family what had happened to their relation.

The ship boy ran off and Dory watched as a few moments later, he fought against the flow coming up the gangway to do her bidding. She would watch until he returned, in case he was forgotten and they left without him.

Over the side of the ship, she could see that they were also taking onboard provisions, which were being hoisted on pallets into a cargo hold—one that people were obviously not sleeping in.

Beside them was another ship and people were streaming up the gangway. *The Pearl of the East* the ship was called. It was taking on a great many people carrying whatever they could.

"Going to Shanghai," a man said next to her.

"Shanghai? That's an awfully long way."

"An open port. You don't need a visa to go. Anyone can turn up and take up residence there." He had an Australian accent.

"Really?"

"These poor bastards are having trouble finding anywhere to go. No one wants them. Mexico is giving out visas, but most other countries are being sparing in the visas they hand out. Some will only take the kids and not the parents."

"That's awful." Why couldn't whole families be taken? Who would care for these children? She wished her own country would be more generous, but there was only a small stream of people coming up the gangway compared to the Shanghai ship. Still, some visas were obviously being granted.

Leaning casually on the railing, the man continued. "Everyone here is looking to go somewhere. Many don't care where, I suppose. I'd fuck off to Shanghai too if I had to. Get the fuck out of this shithole."

That was one way of putting it.

Chapter 30

After the madness of Marseille's port, they slipped away from the French coast, down toward the warm air and sparkling waters of the southern Mediterranean. In a way, it felt as though they were leaving the madness behind, even though that wasn't possibly true.

Even Dory worried about Vivian—not that he would appreciate it. He was so close to where the fighting was. Still, no news had come of the Germans invading Switzerland. In saying that, there had technically been enough time for him to return to the Cote d'Azur, but he hadn't. Perhaps taking someone out of a sanitorium wasn't a straightforward affair, even in wartime.

Then again, he couldn't bring his mother to this boat. Lady Wallisford could not return to the UK. She was effectively in exile—a longstanding tradition for aristocratic criminals.

It was a few days after they left Marseille that Dory spotted Terry Wilcott. He was standing by the railing, smoking while talking to some men, his other hand tucked leisurely in his pocket. He looked as if he hadn't a worry in the world.

Looking over, he caught her watching and waved. They hadn't exactly been friends, but he now acknowledged her. Stuck on this boat, difference in position didn't seem to matter so much. They were in this together, suffering from being transported like livestock.

Was Terry, with his round face and soft eyes, really capable of killing someone—his friend? Livinia said absolutely not, and she had known him a long while. If the land in Palestine was valueless, then there was very little tying Terry to Drecsay in terms of motive. It was just this supposed cartographer that served as an indication that there was more to this story—this land in Palestine.

Quickly, Dory waved back, but she didn't approach. It felt disingenuous being overtly friendly to someone when she was investigating them for murder.

Perhaps it was time to talk to Charlotte. Initially, it had seemed like a good idea, but now, Dory wasn't as convinced that it would tell them any more than they already knew, but it was still worth finding out.

Returning to their area of the boat, she found Livinia who had taken to her role as ship's librarian, having set up a reading corner with makeshift bookshelves she had forced the crewmen to find and retrieve for her. Likely, there wasn't anything she couldn't bully them into doing, speaking with such authority that dissension bordered on traitorous.

"Now, where can we find Charlotte?" Dory asked as she approached Livinia, who was stacking returned books on her shelves. She'd even managed to find a carpet for the reading nook. God knew where she'd got that from.

"Oh, I'll show you. Are you going to interrogate her?"

"I don't interrogate."

"You really haven't heard yourself, then."

Dory opened her mouth to argue, but had to concede that she might not have a leg to stand on. All she did was ask questions. Perhaps some saw it as interrogating. It wasn't, after all, a new accusation. "Fine, I am going to grill her until she squeals like a cornered rat."

Livinia laughed. "Charlotte won't know what's hit her."

At no point had Dory realized there were so many corridors on this ship, and for some reason, Livinia had done a thorough survey of the whole ship. Walking endlessly through areas Dory had never been, they came to a strange compartment where a group of people had set up their quarters. Sheets were hung to provide some semblance of privacy.

"Knock, knock," Livinia said and pushed back a sheet. "Charlotte. Are you in?"

"Here," a woman said, appearing with a book in her hand. Was Livinia bullying people into reading as well? Dory wouldn't put it past her. "Oh, Livinia, what a pleasant surprise. I would invite you to sit, but there is nowhere to sit." The woman's gaze traveled over Dory and she looked back expectantly for an introduction. They had met before. Charlotte obviously didn't remember her. Charlotte was about the same age, and there were similarities between the girls in the way they dressed. Similar type of schooling, Dory would guess.

"This is Dory, Auntie's companion. Remember how you mentioned you saw that man coming from Palestine speaking to Baron Drecsay—cartographer, you said."

"Yes," Charlotte answered. "That's right."

"Now what made you think he was a cartographer?" Livinia asked.

"Well, he had maps. Tons of maps. Some he'd obviously drawn himself."

"He didn't actually say?"

"I didn't actually speak to him. He was only there, around, you know."

"Was anyone else there?" Dory asked.

"It was a café so there were loads of people coming and going every minute, I expect." These questions obviously seemed absurd to Charlotte.

"But anyone you know?"

A slight shrug said no. "No one I noticed."

"How about Terry Wilcott?"

"Why would Terry Wilcott be there? I suppose he and Drecsay were friends, but no, I didn't see Terry there."

"What about at Lady Tonbridge's party?"

Charlotte's expression changed and she looked Dory up and down. Maybe Dory did interrogate people. She didn't seem to be able to ask things casually. That was something she should work on.

"Uhmm," Charlotte tried to think. "I can't quite recall. I saw you dancing with Drecsay, though," Charlotte said while slightly nudging Livinia's arm. "You two seemed to be cozy in each other's company."

"Just friends," Livinia said dismissively.

"I'm sure you got interrogated a time or two about it by the police. You did find him. Whacked on the head. It was bloody from what I hear. I didn't see it myself." There was a certain excited glee in Charlotte's eyes. "I would have been beside myself."

"Yes, it was dreadful," Livinia said coldly and an uncomfortable silence descended.

"Shame," Charlotte said after a while. "He was such a handsome man."

"Do you recall what this cartographer looked like? A name even?"

Charlotte blinked a couple of times. "Average height. Brown hair. Nothing remarkable."

"Age?"

"Young. In his twenties."

"Accent."

"Oh, I think more Oxford than Cambridge, if I were to hazard a guess."

"So he was… " She was going to say 'one of your kind,' but stopped herself, "educated."

"Naturally," Charlotte said as if it was obvious. "John Lobb boots, I'm sure of it. His jacket was obviously Saville Row. Could be Italian, but that would be a stretch."

"No name?"

"We weren't introduced." Charlotte's patience had run out. "I can't believe how hot it's getting. We get no air in here whatsoever, packed in like cattle. It's a disgrace. I should have gone with Stu and driven to Spain. It would have been much more comfortable. I can't believe we have to survive weeks of this." Bringing up her hand, she fanned herself with the book. "And we get nothing to eat but bread and soup. We're all going to starve by the time we reach England."

"We hadn't even considered bringing more from the stores at Villa Bellevieu. Didn't even think about it. If I would have known what this would be like, I would have stuffed my trunk full of food."

It would probably have served them all better if she had.

"Thank you so much for answering our questions," Livinia said, taking Charlotte's hand. "It's been immensely helpful."

"Always glad to help. Are you going to come have a spot of tea with us later? We're trying to make it a regular thing."

"Of course I will."

The invitation was not extended to Dory, which suited her just fine.

"I better get back," Livinia said, urging Dory with her. "She could pick up a man in a line up based entirely on the stitching of his clothes. "But interestingly, as they are John Lobb boots, and I would trust her assessment on that, it is likely the manufacturer could provide us with a name. Perhaps I should get a more accurate description of the boots from her later," Livinia finished absently. She stopped and Dory did too. "I told you that there is no way that Terry would have anything to do with this." She was watching Dory intently now.

"Yes, but that being the case, we need to ensure all the 'I's are dotted and 'T's crossed, otherwise the suspicion would naturally fall on him," Dory said, not feeling the certainty she spoke with. There was technically no evidence to any of this. The only mention of this prospector type was, according to Charlotte's assertion, identified entirely on the clothes he was wearing.

Dory could just imagine how impressed DI Ridley would be if she told him of this supposed 'evidence'. Livinia had at one point asserted that Terry was inordinately unlucky, and being the recipient of a useless piece of land attached to a murder would be seen as the height of bad luck.

There was nothing to say that this prospector had told Drecsay anything. All they really knew was that the man had shown maps. They assumed that Drecsay had purchased the property as a result. There was also no evidence linking Terry to any of this. He was friends with Drecsay—Drecsay owed him money, but he owed other people too, including his other supposed friend Prince Barenoli. They both technically gained by his death through their liens. And of the two of them, Barenoli was the darker character. Terry seemed more good-natured and fun-loving, while Barenoli disdained the world. Both had been at Lady Tonbridge's party. Both liens were resolved with the baron's death. And the apartment, on the surface, was worth much more than this distant land in the desert—but why had Drecsay bought it?

Chapter 31

The coast of Spain was beautiful and a lovely distraction from the ship, where lack of facilities was starting to show in frayed nerves, poorer hygiene, and unruly hair. The rooms were all gradually growing smellier and sniping words were increasingly common.

Dory stood by the railing and watched the Spanish coast slowly glide past. They were too far away to see any life, but they saw buildings, fishing harbors and golden beaches. Well, she had never had the opportunity to go to Spain, but now, she had certainly seen it. The war hadn't reached here and Franco seemed determined to stay out of it. Perhaps that meant there would be something left of it at the end of all this, as the rabble of the German Army seemed to destroy whatever they touched.

The war would end one day. It had to. The Great War had lasted four years. Four years seemed like an impossibly long period of time. Back in history, there was both a thirty-year war and a hundred-year war. The outlook was depressing now that a diplomatic solution seemed less and less likely.

News had filtered through from the people embarking at Marseilles that the Italians had entered the fray by declaring war on both England and France. The news had utterly deflated Dory. Their little safe haven at Villa Bellevieu hadn't been safe at all. For all they knew, it could be run over by Italian soldiers as they spoke. Dory feared for all the people in the village, dreading to think the

Italians were as callous and harmful as the Germans. Every corner of the world seemed under attack.

Now that they were at sea, they heard nothing. There was no news about what was happening in the world, which seemed to rewrite itself every single day. But they were sailing away from harm's way, in the nick of time, too.

Over the next few days, they sailed closer and closer to the Spanish coast, eventually seeing Gibraltar in the distance. British territory. There had been no communication about whether they would be allowed to get off or not.

How nice it would be to wander around the streets for a while and do normal things like sit in a café, or browse through shops. It seemed so long ago since she had done something like that. The British Government probably didn't want a thousand people wandering around the streets of Gibraltar with the burden of having to deal with them if they didn't make it back to the ship on time.

Dory was right. They weren't let off and some took the news badly, arguing with the crewmen, saying they needed this or that. Some had legitimate reasons, saying they needed medicines from the pharmacy. There was a doctor on the ship—a very busy doctor, charged with the care of seven hundred some people who were on this ship.

More were coming on, a small and orderly queue of Gibaltarese. Or where they Gibraltarians? Dory didn't know. She also didn't know if they were better off here than back in Britain, but then Gibraltar was always in a strategic position at the mouth of the Mediterranean. It could be that at some point, it became a focal point. Like everyone else, she was trying to determine where would be a safe location as this war progressed. Out of two locations, which would be safer?

By the look of the small crowd waiting to come on the boat, they had decided that Gibraltar wasn't the better of the options available to them. Or maybe they had other reasons to come. There was a Navy ship in the harbor as well, and mariners moved around the port, all seemingly having a task and a purpose.

With a sigh, she watched as provisions were hauled onto the ship again. Managing this ship wasn't a pretty affair. Latrines had been set up along the ship and they had to be emptied overboard every day. A commissary had been set up for purchasing cigarettes and lozenges. It was all they had. Perhaps after this stop, the commissary would have more.

There would be at least ten more days of this. All of them too close for comfort, an absolute lack of privacy and barely enough water for anyone to wash. Lady Pettifer hardly ever left her bunk, while Livinia made herself busy as responsible for the pursuits of higher learning or simply distraction through her library.

Some of the children did put on plays, which were lovely, and probably the best thing about the whole voyage. The only privacy available was gazing out at sea or the distant coast and trying to forget where one was.

"Miss Dory Sparks," she heard a boy call as he walked along the passageway. "Miss Dory Sparks."

"Here," Dory said and held up her hand. People stood aside from her and the boy approached.

"Telegram," he said and handed over a triple-folded paper.

"Thank you," she said, but the boy was gone the moment he was relieved of his burden.

It opened to a printed form with ticket tape glued in the message section.

COPPER MINING LICENSE WITH COLONIAL OFFICE STOP PAYED BY CHEQUE STOP DRAWER TERRY WILCOTT STOP

Dory gasped. This was the link. Terry Wilcott had paid for the mining license for the property. It was all registered and he had paid by cheque. There was no doubt that he knew about the baron's plans and the economic potential of this land. Terry had been a part of the planning. He'd even paid with a cheque from his account. Surely, he could not have intended to kill at that point as there was a clear link between him and the motive.

On flying feet, Dory made her way to their little cabin, where Lady Pettifer was leaning back on their scant pillows and drinking tea.

"Telegram from Ridley," she said and held it out to Lady Pettifer.

After reading it, she looked up. "We have him," Lady Pettifer said. "As much as by lying about it, he admits his culpability."

Lady Pettifer sighed and put the note down on her lap.

"Now what?" Dory asked. "Should we tell the Captain?"

"Now things are complicated. We know he did it, but what jurisdiction is there to do something? Away from France and the people officially responsible for the investigation, there is little we can do. I think we must perhaps talk to the Captain and apprise him of the situation. Whether he can act on this information, we will have to see. The question is if Terry Wilcott presents a danger to anyone else. For now, we know exactly where he is. It may be that we have to leave this until we reach the UK."

"Alright, we'll see the Captain. Should we see him now before we leave port?"

"Yes, probably. Help me up."

Dory moved to assist Lady Pettifer rise from the bunk. It was an unnatural position for her to get up from, dodging Livinia's bunk as she did.

They walked toward where the bridge of the ship was, gingerly stepping over people in their little make-do camps along every available surface. The door to the bridge was gray metal with rounded edges. They had to knock and eventually a uniformed man appeared, eyeing them suspiciously.

"We need to see the Captain," Lady Pettifer said.

"The Captain is busy at the moment," the man said, preparing to close the door.

"It is a matter of some urgency."

"The ship steward is tasked with handling passenger queries."

It was a joke making out like this ship was designed to deal with passengers in any regard.

"This regards a crime," Lady Pettifer said in her most grave voice that only a lady of the aristocracy could pull off. As expected, it made the man waiver. Lady Pettifer had a forcefulness when she needed it, a communication of authority that only persons of equal authority could face down. "As I said, it is a matter of urgency in light of our imminent departure."

The man weakened. "I will speak to the Captain and see if he will see you."

Lady Pettifer didn't waver in her expectation and the man walked away. A few moments later, the Captain appeared. He wore a dark blue jacket with gold stripes around the cuffs. With his neatly trimmed gray beard, he did look the part. He had to be uncomfortable in this heat in that jacket.

"How may I be of assistance, madam?" the man said dryly.

"I am Lady Pettifer, and certain queries have brought to light the fact that we have a murderer onboard."

The Captain's eyebrows rose, but he didn't look entirely convinced. "Was this a crime that occurred on this ship?"

"No, it occurred in France."

The man was silent for a moment. "That makes things rather tricky as we are now in a British port. Do you have some evidence of this?"

Dory handed over the telegram to the Captain, who looked at it. Obviously, he wouldn't get any understanding from that.

"This telegram establishes the motive, and shows clearly that he has been lying to us. It was sent by a DI Ridley from the Met."

The Captain looked at the telegram again. "It doesn't say so."

"Are you suggesting I'm lying?" Lady Pettifer demanded.

"I am suggesting nothing of the sort, but you have to understand that it would be hard to arrest a man for a crime based on this... evidence. If we called in the Gibraltarian Police, they could only hold him for so long, having no body, no investigation, based on supposed evidence of a DI in the UK. I am, of course, not an expert at this, but I don't expect they could pull together sufficient evidence in time involving such a complex case. It may be better to deliver this man to the UK, where the evidence against him is assembled."

It struck Dory that they didn't even have that. DI Ridley didn't have a case against this man—that was the Gendarmerie in France. The baron wasn't even a British citizen. It was even more complicated than the Captain assumed. Their option was to have him arrested here, where he would assuredly be released in a matter of days due to lack of evidence, to then slip across the border to wherever he wished, or to keep him on the ship where he would be delivered to England.

Unfortunately, this case was too complex legally for any of the assembled party to deal with, Dory realized.

"Under the circumstances, it is perhaps best that DI Ridley deal with this. But be aware of the situation and this man's presence onboard the ship," Lady Pettifer ordered.

"Mr. Terry Wilcott, I take it," the Captain said. "It may be best to keep this information under our hats. Panic is never a good thing on a ship."

"Noted," Lady Pettifer said. "I need to send a telegram."

The man eyed her harshly. "We are just about to leave."

"As we have agreed this investigation and arrest is too complicated for us to deal with here. I would like to send a telegram to the Commissioner of Police. He is an associate of my brothers."

"Tom," the Captain said back into the bridge. A boy appeared. "Get this lady a piece of paper and then deliver it to the Harbor Master to send. Quick as you can, boy."

A paper was found and Lady Pettifer dictated as Dory crouched to the floor and wrote. The boy sprinted away.

"I suggest you stay out of this man's way during the rest of this journey," the Captain said.

With a nod, Lady Pettifer took her leave. They walked over to the ship's starboard side and watched the boy run down the gangway, which was just about to be retracted. The waiting crowd must have embarked already and they were ready to leave. The boy handed the note to one of the men working on the dock.

"Not sure that telegram will ever reach the Commissioner," Lady Pettifer said. "Unfortunately, the Captain is right. A body in France during a war, and a culprit fleeing the country makes everything very complicated. As in France, no one has the resources to see to something like this right now. But if that telegram does reach the Commissioner, he would be duty bound to act. What he will achieve remains to be seen."

"He will do what he can, I'm sure," Dory said. The Commissioner would not come up with some civilized solution as he had for Lady Wallisford in sending her to Switzerland, Dory was sure. Extradition was hard under normal circumstances. During a war, it might be impossible.

Chapter 32

Dory felt strangely deflated when they got back to the cabin. The murder had been solved, the culprit identified. The fact that they couldn't do anything about it was out of her hands. She'd done her part. Baron Drecsay didn't perhaps have his revenge, or even justice, but what had happened to him was now known, and would continue to be so. His family would be told why he died, and hopefully that would be some comfort to them.

"I suppose we have done what we can," Lady Pettifer said as she sat down heavily on the bunk again. "The greed is just unfathomable. I think I will have a little lie-down."

Livinia appeared at the door. "It is said they're selling coffee granules in the commissary."

Coffee would make the next week much more tolerable. "I think I will go buy us some before it's all gone."

"I can't believe how excited we are getting about some coffee granules that we would normally think were undrinkable."

"I don't mind the granules." Dory said.

"Well, you wouldn't."

Thank you, Livinia, Dory thought through gritted teeth. It was easy to get offended by the things Livinia said, but living with her for the last two years had taught Dory that Livinia was largely unintentionally rude. She simply stated whatever entered her mind, and to her simply a statement of fact. As granulated coffee was cheaper and easy to make without the assistance of skilled staff, it would go to show that Dory, being from a more modest background, would like the taste as if it was what she was used to. To Livinia, that was pure logic.

Picking up her coin purse, Dory excused herself and walked toward the walkway along the port side of the ship. The commissary was on the other end of the ship and anything they had picked up from Gibraltar would find interested buyers before long. If Dory wanted coffee, she had to get some now.

The sun was very bright on this side of the ship. Heat radiating from the painted steel added to the sun's harsh rays. There were people who shifted their daytime camps from the different sides of the ship depending on the time of day, seeking shade during the warmest hours.

Right now, this side was largely deserted. Walking past a protrusion, which narrowed the walkway considerably. Just past it, she saw Terry standing next to the railing, leaning casually. He looked up as Dory walked around the protrusion.

"Miss Sparks," Terry said with a broad smile. "Going for a walk? One does need to stretch one's legs on this journey. It is cramped, isn't it?"

"It is not the most comfortable, but the times are dire."

"They are, aren't they?" Terry pushed off the railing where he was leaning. There was something uncomfortable about this. Dory took a step back. "I was wondering," he started as he moved closer. He was still smiling and his stance wasn't particularly aggressive. "Must be on your way to the commissary, I'm guessing. I am, too."

"This isn't near where you are staying."

"Oh, you know where I am staying. Keeping tabs on me?"

"I just assumed. I saw you down the other end of the ship, so I assumed you were staying down that way."

"Assumptions can be dangerous."

That was enough for Dory. His actions weren't overtly aggressive, but he'd even used the word 'dangerous'. "I better go check on... Livinia."

"See, I know you've been asking things you shouldn't. Just can't leave things alone, can you?"

Dory went to briskly walk back the way she had come. They were virtually unseen here. Granted, there were a few people on the story above. Dory could see their arms sticking out over the railing, but they weren't watching.

Suddenly, she got yanked back. He had her by the hair. "You should have just left things alone."

"Let go of me, Terry," she stated, trying to pull away, but he was deceptively strong.

"I just can't let you ruin everything. Nothing personal, Miss Sparks, but you have an incessant habit of sticking your nose where it doesn't belong."

"Let go," Dory repeated, feeling panic flare up inside. Terry pulled her back and over. Dory grabbed the railing in a death grip as Terry's arms snaked around her. His intentions were clear now. He was going to lift her over. With all her might, she pushed back against him as he tried to manhandle her closer to the railing.

Images of her falling into the water filled her mind. They were quite far from the shore now, but there was a chance she could swim back. Thank God she knew how to swim.

"You don't really think throwing me overboard will cover up what you did. More than I know what you did."

"You mean the old crone. I'm sure I can find some way to convince her."

"Then you don't know the lady in the least."

"I can be persuasive. You know, I never wanted any of this. You brought this on by simply not letting it go."

"You killed someone. You killed your friend."

A blow to her head made Dory's vision waiver. If she passed out, she would be over the railing in a heartbeat, drowning in mere seconds. The last thing she could afford right now was to lose consciousness.

Wrenching herself away, she tried to run, but it only gave him more leverage to lift her up, and now she had no grip. She had no way to thwart him in his intentions to hoist her over the side.

There was a thud and she was falling. Panic speared through every thought she had, but he was short, she wasn't over the railing, was falling into it. Then a clear gong just before Dory's shoulder hit against the solid steel of the railing wall. Pain flared across her entire back.

"Terry, you blasted miscreant," Livinia shouted. As Dory looked up, she saw Livinia standing with two books in her hands, ready to strike again. Terry lay with his arm and half his body over Dory—the dead weight was hard to shift, but with all her effort, Dory managed to get out and away.

Splayed face down, he lay unconscious. The gong she'd heard must have been Terry's head hitting the railing.

"You killed him, you sorry bastard," Livinia said, kicking him harshly. The force of it moved him, but he was still unconscious. Others had started to arrive, drawn by the commotion and they stood around, watching agape as Livinia moved to strike him with the books again.

"No," Dory said, moving to intercept her. "They'll arrest him. He needs to be arrested," Dory said, turning her attention to the crowd. A group of men moved in and lifted Terry up by the arms. They dragged him away and at that point, Dory didn't care where as long as he was away from her.

Her heart was still pounding powerfully inside her chest. She'd been very close to being thrown in the sea and left behind. There was a good chance that no one would notice, and it would take hours before anyone confirmed that she was missing from the ship. If it hadn't been for Livinia and her ability to strike true, Dory would be in the sea by now.

"Thank you," she said, her voice breathy.

"I can't believe it. Terry. Why would he do such an awful thing?"

"Money," Dory said. "Plain and simple. He killed Drecsay so he could steal the land in Palestine."

"Why?" Livinia demanded.

"There was copper beneath that land, apparently."

Livinia's face crumpled and her eyes grew glassy. "Drecsay died for a cheap robbery."

"Basically." It seemed Livinia was cut to pieces over Drecsay's death. There really wasn't the point in telling her that he'd been using her. Now Livinia's purpose seemed logical. Both Dory and Lady Pettifer had assumed that Livinia had been the means to which Drecsay would restore the family wealth. An heiress is usually sought for that purpose, but that wasn't his main project. So why the interest in Livinia? It could be that he simply liked her, but for some reason that didn't sit right. An alternative reason would be that he needed money to set up the mine. That had been Livinia's purpose. Drecsay was set to capitalize his mine in exchange for marriage and his title.

The man still wasn't good enough for Livinia, who had never seen the pure commercial aspect of the bargain— and for that, Drecsay didn't deserve someone like Livinia.

As for herself, Terry had just tried to murder her. The reality was only hitting Dory now and she felt her knees weaken. She needed to sit down. "Let's return to the cabin," she said in a shaky voice. In all, she had been useless in a fight against an assailant. If it hadn't been for Livinia, things would not have resolved so well.

People parted as they walked past. In a way, Dory didn't want to tell Lady Pettifer what had happened, because she knew the elderly lady would take responsibility for it, for allowing Dory to put herself in danger. This wasn't Lady Pettifer's fault. It wasn't Dory's fault. It was Terry's fault.

Mischief in St. Tropez

Chapter 33

Nearly every person on the ship was standing along the walkways as they neared the coast of Cornwall. It was still a fraught portion of the journey, where there was no guarantee that they wouldn't meet a German submarine confusing them for a military ship. It did happen. Everyone had heard of the merchant ships that had been sunk by German submarines earlier in the year. And this looked like a merchant ship if one ever did.

But they had reached the coast, which made people hope that they were safe. Surely the Germans wouldn't strike this close to the shore, but Dory honestly didn't see a reason why that would put them off. At least they were close enough to swim to land, one person had said. A sinking ship with close to eight hundred people was never going to end well.

The other ship was in sight not far behind them. So far, they were both afloat, and approaching Southampton. Another day and they would be there.

After Terry Wilcott's attempt on her life, he'd been imprisoned in the brig. It was nothing more than a cabin whose residents had grudgingly been evicted, but Terry was locked in there for the rest of the voyage. Dory wasn't sure what would happen to him now, but in a way, she didn't care. To her, it felt as though her part had been completed. It was up to others now to do what they did. Anything beyond this would be out of her hands. No doubt, she would at some point be called to testify in a hearing against him. It may even be in France. As to when, she couldn't even guess.

Even Lady Pettifer came out of the cabin for the celebration for reaching the English coastline. This journey had been hard on her and she had quietly suffered through most of it. It didn't do her body well to stay in such cramped quarters with barely enough room to move, and everywhere else was so full of obstacles, it was simply easier for her to stay put.

Mr. Fernley had done his best to serve, but there wasn't room for him or really the need. Every day, he came with Lady Pettifer's meals on a tray, then disappeared to wherever he'd found space on the ship. Dory had gotten the distinct feeling he hadn't liked this trip much either. Beauty, who was confined to her crate had to despise it, but there wasn't much for it.

The ship was also running out of water, which had been distressing. Now they were slowly floating past the coast of Cornwall. The end was in sight.

"I do hope George is here with the car," Lady Pettifer said. Livinia stood on the other side of her, quiet for a change. George was Lord Wallisford's driver, and a name Dory hadn't heard for over two years. Her months serving as a maid at Wallisford Hall seemed a lifetime ago. "Shall you come back with us?" Lady Pettifer's attention was on Dory.

There had been considerable time on the ship to consider this question. "No, I think I need to go see my mother in Swanley." Lady Pettifer had no need for a companion here in England, and the thought of going back to Wallisford Hall sat uncomfortably. As Lady Pettifer's companion, she would be given one of the guestrooms and then be served as a guest by the people she used to work with—the people who had made things very difficult for her when she had helped DI Ridley uncover what Lady Wallisford had done. All in all, it would be an uncomfortable affair.

It was time to move onto whatever came next in her life. The close friendship with Lady Pettifer was the hardest thing to let go of. It was what she treasured. Everything else... it was time to put it behind her.

"What will you do?" Lady Pettifer asked.

"I don't know yet. Women are needed for all sorts of jobs, I understand. I am sure they will find some use for me."

"It is true that you will be of more service to the country away from Wallisford Hall. I suppose at times like these, we cannot keep hold of our companions, even if we want to." Putting her arm around Lady Pettifer, Dory squeezed her shoulder. "I honestly have no idea what kind of country we are returning to. I wonder if this war is shaping up to be very different from the last. Still, the country will be run by women, I suppose. I am sure you will be needed. Perhaps you will even be a policeman. I think you do have a knack for it. You too, Livinia. You are going to have to find some way of being useful."

"Not sure my skills will be all that valued," Livinia said.

"Considering that you speak both French and German, I think they will find something for you to do."

"Do you think they'll send me as a spy?" she said humorously.

"I don't think you could hide the fact that you are British even if you tried."

"I might stay in London for a while. See what everyone is doing," Livinia said. The Wallisford family had a townhouse, but Dory didn't exactly know where.

"Your father will want to see you. You have been gone two years," Lady Pettifer pointed out and her tone carried her disapproval.

"Yes, I suppose I will have to go see daddy first," Livinia admitted. "He should be at the hall this time of year."

"If George is there, we can drop you off in Swanley," Lady Pettifer continued.

"I am sure it will be out of your way," Dory said.

"Nonsense. We have traveled this far together, a few more miles isn't going to hurt anyone."

It was strange to think she was going home to Swanley. It had been so long since she'd been back. With the difficulty with mail lately, it had even been hard to get letters through.

"To whatever the future holds for us," Dory said and they all looked out at the passing coastline. Sunshine basked the rugged, dark green landscape, interspersed with white beaches. It was a part of the country Dory hadn't seen until she had sailed to France two years back. There was so much of the world she hadn't seen—so much of Britain she hadn't seen. She'd never even been to Scotland.

In truth, she had no idea where she would end up. It felt a little like she was leaving it up to fate. In a way, it was quite scary. She had found a really comfortable place with Lady Pettifer, but she was too young to hide away in comfort in someone else's house. There was too much to be done, too much to be explored. From the start, she'd known this time would come and now it was here.

*

They moved away from the coastline and toward the Isle of Wight. They were nearing their destination. Lunch had been yet another meal of the tasteless, ubiquitous soup. Dory's mouth watered for a proper meal. Tonight, she would dine at her mother's house. The thought of her mother's cooking made her smile. She might not be the cook that Gladys was, but she made a lovely supper.

They were outside again, watching as they sailed past the Isle of Wight. This ship had carried them all the way home. Anxiousness and anticipation were growing around them. Everyone had packed their belongings and were ready to disembark. Dory knew that a few of these people had nowhere to go, had lost ties with England, lost family and friends over time. They would have to find a place for themselves until they could return to their adopted country, who didn't want them in this time of war.

Dory's thoughts turned back to Prince Barenoli, wondering that solution he had found for himself. With the Italians pressing on the border, he had to go somewhere. They might even have invaded for all they knew. There was no news on the ship. By the look of the peaceful Isle of

Wight, it seemed the world hadn't ended while they had been afloat along the Atlantic Ocean.

A while later, they sailed past the naval base in Portsmouth, but they were not stopping there. Technically a merchant ship, they kept going to Southampton, where cars were waiting patiently beside the dock they seemed intent for. Southampton port had none of the chaotic scenes in France. Cars were waiting for people. There were other ships around, unloading their pallets of cargo. American by the look of them. They were still getting supplies from America, it seemed.

The lack of chaos was encouraging. Things could not be so bad if no one was desperately fleeing. This was where many wished to flee to, including them.

They felt it in the structure of the ship as the engine slowed, and tugs appeared, working to guide them. It was hard to imagine those little boats being powerful enough to maneuver such a large ship.

Foremost at the dock was a police car and a group of men was standing around—one in uniform. Dory knew instantly that it was DI Ridley and she felt her heart beat powerfully in her chest. He had come—here to arrest Terry.

"Seems your DI is here," Lady Pettifer said.

"He's not my DI," Dory said, flaring red.

"Is there some tenderness between you and that policeman?" Livinia asked. "I never knew."

"Of course not," Dory said, but she knew neither of them believed her. Maybe she didn't entirely believe it either, considering her hands were clammy and a nervousness had set itself deep in her belly.

"They will lead Terry off first. Perhaps you should follow and speak to the good DI. I am sure he will wish to see you before he takes Terry away," Lady Pettifer said.

"Yes, perhaps you are right," Dory said, feeling flustered.

"Go on. We'll see you down on the dock after."

"I am going to have to carry my trunk myself, aren't I?" Livinia said as Dory walked away.

The gangway was a story down and Dory had to fight her way past people who were already lined up. The Captain was standing by the opening to the gangway with some of his sailors, firmly keeping Terry Wilcott in custody.

Dory decided to stay back a little, unwilling to provoke an interaction with Terry. The fact that he hated her was beyond doubt, and there was nothing to be gained by speaking to him. So, she waited. The gangway made grinding, mechanical sounds as it was extended into place, and the gate finally opened. The Captain and his men walked Terry down to the waiting policemen. Dory pushed through to follow, but the crowd surged forward in their eagerness for firm land.

It took a few minutes, but Dory finally made it onto the gangway and started descending, holding her small suitcase in her hand.

DI looked up and saw her, a smile gracing his lips. Her throat went dry as she moved closer. "I heard there was a scuffle," he said when she stepped down on the ground.

"Yes," she admitted.

"You will have to press charges. The murder will be hard to deal with at a time like this, but attacking you, he will stand trial for."

DI Ridley wore a green uniform instead of his typical suit. He was in his military gear, she realized. He seemed to notice her observation. "I am only here temporarily. I need to head back to Pirbright almost immediately. I only came for the arrest."

"Of course," Dory said with a smile. "Thank you."

"Don't thank me. I am not happy to hear he attacked you."

"Livinia Fellingworth saved the day, would you believe it?"

DI Ridley didn't see the humor in it and Dory wiped the smile from her face.

"Where are you heading?" he asked.

"To Swanley."

People were streaming down the gangway behind them, and Terry was seated in the back of the police car with men guarding him. He was resolutely staring straight ahead, a tight expression of displeasure on his mouth. His displeasure wasn't going to change any of the things that were about to happen to him, and he deserved whatever punishment was meted out. Dory turned away and refused to think about him more. He didn't deserve it.

"I can drive you as far as Pirbright, but I can't take you all the way. I only have a few hours," Ridley said, checking his watch.

There were so many things Dory wanted to say and ask, but it wasn't the place for it.

"Lady Pettifer," he said, moving his attention away from Dory. Dory almost felt the pressure of his gaze let. "I am glad to see you've found your way back to England."

"It wasn't a comfortable journey, but these are dire times."

"Yes, they are," he said. It was discouraging to hear him say that, but there was no hiding they were at war.

"Lady Pettifer has offered to drive me home," Dory said.

"Good. It can be hard getting passage, particularly down toward Dover way. Have a safe journey. Watch out for the trucks on the road."

"We will," Lady Pettifer said. "I saw George over to the left. It seemed my brother has not forgotten that we are arriving."

The police car started and DI Ridley gave them a nod, before turning his attention back to Dory. "I will write to inform you what happens from here. You will have to testify in court. I will be there if I can, but I might not be able to. My schedule is… uncertain, but you can reach me at Pirbright if you have any questions. They can forward letters if need be. Miss Sparks," he said with a quick nod before he walked over to the police car and got in next to the driver.

They quickly drove away down the dock, which was now crowded with families reunited.

"The uniform certainly becomes him, doesn't it?" Livinia said. "I think you should definitely come up with some questions to ask him."

Dory blushed but refused to look back. She cleared her throat. "Where was it you saw George?"

"Yes," Livinia said, stretching to look around. "I need him to go get my trunk. It was simply too heavy to lift."

The End

Next book in the Dory Sparks Mysteries series

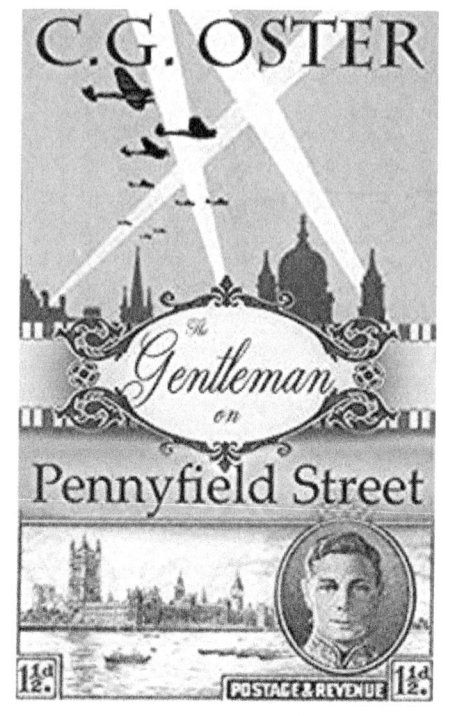

The Gentleman at Pennyfield Street – As the German planes came, London burned. Like everyone else, Dory had a job to do, searching for the threat that came in the night sky. Night after night, she and Vera searched for the enemy, while the bombs fell on street after street. The dark and empty streets of London also concealed the worst of intentions in the rubble and chaos of a blighted city—a perfect place to hide a murder.

Mischief in St. Tropez